A CANDLELIGHT ROMANCE

CANDLELIGHT ROMANCES

182 Dangerous Assignment, JENNIFER BLAIR
183 Walk a Dark Road, LYNN WILLIAMS
184 Counterfeit Love, JACQUELYN AEBY
185 The Gentleman Pirate, JANETTE RADCLIFFE
186 The Golden Falcon, BETTY HALE HYATT
187 Tower in the Forest, ETHEL HAMILL
188 Master of Roxton, ELISABETH BARR
189 The Steady Flame, BETH MYERS
190 White Jasmine, JANETTE RADCLIFFE
191 Cottage on Catherina Cay, JACQUELYN AEBY
192 Quest for Alexis, NANCY BUCKINGHAM
193 Falconer's Hall, JACQUELYN AEBY
194 Shadows of Amanda, HELEN S. NUELLE
195 The Long Shadow, JENNIFER BLAIR
196 Portrait of Errin, BETTY HALE HYATT
197 A Dream of Her Own, MARYANN YOUNG
198 Lord Stephen's Lady, JANETTE RADCLIFFE
199 The Storm, JACQUELYN AEBY
200 Dr. Myra Comes Home, ARLENE HALE
201 Winter in a Dark Land, MIRIAM LYNCH
202 The Sign of the Blue Dragon, JACQUELYN AEBY
203 A Happy Ending, ARLENE HALE
204 The Azure Castle, JANETTE RADCLIFFE
205 Never Look Back, JACQUELYN AEBY
206 The Topaz Charm, JANETTE RADCLIFFE
207 Teach Me To Love, GAIL EVERETT
208 The Brigand's Bride, BETTY HALE HYATT
209 Share Your Heart, ARLENE HALE
210 The Gallant Spy, BETTY HALE HYATT
211 Love is the Winner, GAIL EVERETT
212 Scarlet Secrets, JANETTE RADCLIFFE
213 Revelry Manor, ELISABETH BARR
214 Pandora's Box, BETTY HALE HYATT
215 Safe Harbor, JENNIFER BLAIR
216 A Gift of Violets, JANETTE RADCLIFFE
217 Stranger on the Beach, ARLENE HALE
218 To Last a Lifetime, JENNIFER BLAIR
219 The Way to the Heart, GAIL EVERETT
220 Nurse in Residence, ARLENE HALE
221 The Raven Sisters, DOROTHY MACK
222 When Dreams Come True, ARLENE HALE
223 When Summer Ends, GAIL EVERETT
224 Love's Surprise, GAIL EVERETT

Hold Me Forever

MELISSA BLAKELY

A CANDLELIGHT ROMANCE

Published by
Dell Publishing Co., Inc.
1 Dag Hammarskjold Plaza
New York, New York 10017

Dell ® TM 681510, Dell Publishing Co., Inc.

ISBN: 0-440-13488-9

Printed in the United States of America

First printing—March 1978

Hold Me Forever

CHAPTER ONE

Dazed, Sally looked about her at the familiar things in the huge old editorial office. Deep green eyes, wide with the news she had just received, traveled over the framed, yellowed front pages, the faded autographed pictures of politicians and baseball stars, the bronze plaque mementos of long-ago journalistic triumphs, and all the sentimental clutter that had accumulated during *The Glenbrook Patriot*'s eighty years of publication. Above her, the ancient ceiling fans, still waiting to be replaced by air conditioning, purred softly in the late summer afternoon.

"Then I guess that's settled, and you will be in New York three weeks from now." The voice beside her brought Sally back abruptly. "My dear girl, I don't have to tell you how proud of you I am. It only remains to be said that I am also grateful." The gnarled old hand patted the slender young one. "Yes, grateful," Cornelius Smith repeated with emphasis when his young companion started to protest.

"You should be proud, Smithy, since I couldn't have done it without you," the girl cut in, laughing up at him, her face flushed with happiness. "But as for gratitude—" she shook her head wordlessly, looking at him with eyes that expressed everything that words could not. Pressing slightly unsteady hands against her temples as if to clear her head, she turned quietly to face him.

"Smithy . . . I . . . I'm just beginning to take in what you've been telling me. It's what I wanted for as long as I can remember and now that I have it, it doesn't seem possible." With astonishment she repeated to herself, savoring the words, "I have a job on *The New York Globe*."

Cornelius Smith, editor of *The Patriot* for more than twenty years, once a giant of a man, and even now at sixty-eight still an imposing figure, looked down at the glowing upturned face, and a wave of tenderness swept over him. He didn't usually feel such affection for one of his reporters but Sally was different. He had known that the first week she had come to the paper, fresh from college, almost three years ago.

Sally was everything that was fetching in a young woman and a damned good writer besides. A born writer, he mused, and after half a century in the business he knew the good ones were born that way; they could never be made.

Smiling down at her fondly, he said, "My dear, you have already repaid me for whatever small favor I was able to do for you." Seeing she was about to protest again, he waved her objection away and continued. "I have always argued that the backbone of American journalism is the small-town paper. Some of this country's most memorable writers began their careers on unhailed little papers."

Walking over to one of the large windows of his office he went on, almost as if addressing the town outside. "God knows, I have had to fight with both fists at times to keep this one going. There were times when I put *The Patriot* to bed at the end of the week and didn't know if its presses would ever roll again."

Strolling back to his massive mahogany desk, which was built like a fortress and had often served him as one, he sat down in a deep leather chair opposite the young reporter. He looked appreciatively at the delicately boned face with its glowing clear complexion, framed by a cloud of honey-colored hair, the sea-green eyes now fixed intently on his face. There was a cool, crisp confidence about her he admired all the more because she still had, in unguarded moments, an air of youthful vulnerability.

"You have proven me right, Sally," he said, reaching out and patting her hand again. Picking up a newspaper from his desk, he said, "This is as fine a piece of reporting as any big-city journalist could have done. Better," he corrected, his old voice full of an excitement it had not held for years, "given their resources compared to our scanty ones."

Sally's eyes lit with pleasure as she looked at the front page of the tabloid for the hundredth time that day.

It was a copy of *The New York Globe*, an afternoon daily with one of the largest circulations and toughest reputations in the country. On its front page was splashed Sally's coverage of a recent mine disaster in a small Pennsylvania town, not far from Glenbrook. At the head of the story, in large type, stood her name: Sally Spencer.

She felt slightly foolish at the effect the sight of her byline had on her. I'm acting like a schoolgirl who has just won first prize for a composition, she scolded herself, but her pleasure did not diminish.

The Globe was owned by the same company as the small weekly *Patriot,* so its editors had felt free to pirate Sally's reporting of the mining tragedy that had attracted nationwide interest. It was no minor triumph for a small-town reporter to get a front-page story in a major metropolitan newspaper. The realization of this, together with the prospect of her new job, overwhelmed her for a moment. Jumping up, she impulsively threw her arms about the old man and cried, "Smithy, I still can't—"

Resorting to the brusque manner he hid behind whenever he was embarrassed, Smithy cut her short. "I've told you it took me only a phone call so don't go wringing your hands at me," he blustered self-consciously. "I still have a little pull left, you know, even in almighty New York. A handful of people still remember me from my days in the town. I rang one of them on *The Globe* and once I told him about you, it was all settled. He already knew how well you could write. Of course," he added with irony, "it helped when I mentioned I knew Rafe Hawker personally." Shaking his head with amusement, he chuckled to himself. "Amazing what even a mention of that man's name can do!"

Rafe Hawker. Sally's thoughts drifted for a moment to one of the most talked-about but least-known men in the country. The very name held power, and among people in the newspaper world it had been shortened to "the Hawk."

Like that bird of prey, he was swift, predatory, and merciless. An enigma and phenomenon at the same time, he had emerged out of no-one-was-sure-where about fifteen years earlier, and began buying up papers all over the country. His deals displayed a mastery of ruthlessness which left his competitors and victims floundering helplessly.

Once a paper was bought by Hawker it was relentlessly pummeled into shape until it was a success—not necessarily a literary success, as his critics pointed out with envious scorn, but always a financial one. At the moment, Hawker Enterprises owned fifty-six papers all over the country. Several were large metropolitan papers, *The New York Globe* being the largest, but dozens were small-town papers which he had bought on the verge of bankruptcy and whipped into shape in a remarkably short time. It was into this category that *The Glenbrook Patriot* fell.

The man was all the more awesome because of the complex mystery surrounding him. Though he was utterly without respect for other people's privacy, as the merciless exposés in his papers proved, his own private life was impenetrable.

Sally knew Smithy had met the publishing magnate

several times and had a lot of respect for him. Now she asked tentatively, "Is Rafe Hawker really the ruthless ogre his reputation implies?"

"Most people in the business like to paint him as such, although I suspect it's mostly envy on their part," Smithy said thoughtfully. "The fact is, Hawker has an uncanny and infallible instinct for what sells newspapers. The man is a relative newcomer to publishing and yet seems to know better than others with years of experience what is needed to bring a dying paper back to life.

"The only policy a Hawker paper pursues faithfully is one of making money, and although a lot of people resent that, it seems to work very successfully." The old man shook his head with admiration. "If it hadn't been for Hawker, *The Patriot* would be nothing but a memory now. I went to him five years ago when it was about to fold and asked him to buy it. It was in very bad shape then. The owners had lost interest and refused to put up any money for the modernizations that were necessary. But Hawker listened to me, recognized a good deal, and bought it. Within three months we had it completely reorganized and it began showing a healthy profit. During my few dealings with him I have always found him courteous, in his own peculiar fashion. He's reasonable and admirably professional."

Suddenly glancing at Sally with concern, he asked, "You're not intimidated by all that gossip about him? Most of that is pure invention, you know, because very few people really know him. And you don't have to worry, you're not likely to meet him even if you work there twenty years. From what I hear, he wisely keeps himself at a distance from his staff.

"Anyway," he added proudly, "the reason you got yourself this job on *The Globe* was the splendid work you did on this story. They couldn't help being impressed."

Sally smiled to herself, knowing this last was some-

thing Smithy had added by way of encouragement.
She knew the Hawker papers were not unduly impressed by good work. They demanded it from their
reporters and paid well for it.

"The truth is, I have been intending to do something
like this for a long time," the old editor continued in
a serious tone, settling back in his chair and lighting a
cigar.

"I've known that sometime soon you would have to
leave here to take your chances on a bigger paper.
Much as I think of small-town journals, as hard as I
have fought for the recognition due them, I do not
delude myself into thinking that they are challenging
enough for someone of your abilities. I have had my
time on big-city papers, as I think any journalist
serious about his work should. That's why, as sad-
dened as I am at the thought of losing you, my dear,
I wholly approve and support your determination to
go to New York.

"This," he added, pointing to the copy of *The Globe*,
"was the very thing we needed to get a foot in the
door." Skimming over the print, he remarked with
approval, "I notice they hardly changed a word of
your story, so your style obviously fits in well with
The Globe's. Don't underestimate the value of that.
You can be the greatest writer in the world but if you
can't adapt your style to fit the paper you work for,
you're useless. I've seen it happen to many writers."

Apprehension crept over Sally for the first time
since Smithy had broken the news to her. What if
she could not do it, if she failed in New York? The
thought chilled her and for a moment she felt a flutter
of fear in the pit of her stomach. It was one thing
to do well in the security of your own hometown,
with the support and encouragement of your family
and colleagues behind you, but quite another to sur-
vive in such a competitive job in such a competitive
city as New York. The thought of that place with its
cold impersonality filled her with panic for an instant.

But determinedly she shook herself free of the uneasy moment. She had wanted this chance, dreamed of it and planned for it for far too long to allow herself to be frightened by it when it dropped right into her lap.

She remembered with satisfaction that from the moment she joined the *Patriot* staff she had been put through her paces thoroughly and was familiar with every function of the paper. From copying down names correctly at a local wedding to taking painstaking notes at the town council's meetings, from editing and rewriting copy to correcting proofs, she had been trained with a firm hand. Whenever some menial task got her down, Smithy had always rallied her with a stern, "Don't sniff at it, it's all good experience. Store it away for the future!" He had been so right, she thought now with gratitude. However formidable New York seemed, she would not be going there totally unprepared.

With an involuntary thrust of her small chin, she got up, her confidence restored.

"Yes, you had better go now and break the news to your family," Smithy said, getting up to walk to the door with her. "I don't know how your Aunt Emily is going to take it," he added, shaking his head. "Now that all the others have left home, she is going to take the loss of the last child mighty hard."

"Hardly a child at twenty-four," Sally protested with a laugh. "I know she will miss me," she agreed with a slight feeling of remorse, "but she knows how much I've wanted this and she will be happy for me."

"Good-bye then, dear. We'll go over the final arrangements after you've talked to the family." The telephone rang in his office so Sally left him at his door with a quick hug and made her way out alone.

For a moment the old man lingered, looking after Sally as she left. There was a spring in her step and a proud lift to her fine head. She looked the picture of natural poise and confidence. And why not? She was young, determined, an exceptionally talented writer, and pretty. Yes, very pretty, he decided, turning to answer the insistent ringing of the telephone.

Sally walked through the empty outer office she had shared with her colleagues for the past two-and-a-half years. It was after six o'clock now and the others had already gone. Fighting the urge to linger there, she skipped lightly down the short flight of stairs, then crossed the lobby in a couple of strides of her long, slim legs, and stood at the entrance, squinting into the orange glow of the evening sun. Hesitating for a moment, she looked along Main Street where the ancient Patriot Building stood. She knew she should be going straight home, but instead she headed in the direction away from her house, oddly reluctant to break the news to her family just yet.

Her thoughts were in something of a turmoil and she wanted them properly sorted out before confronting the family. If her intuitive Aunt Emily suspected that something was troubling her niece, she would work herself into a state of worry. Sally wanted complete control over herself and the strange mixture of elation and trepidation mingling in her heart.

Walking down Main Street, clean and neat as a postcard with its immaculate buildings and flowering gardens so typical of that part of Pennsylvania, she felt a touch of pride in her hometown. She remembered a little shamefully that there had been times when she had almost despised it. Longing to be away and living an exciting life in New York, she had been irritated by its smallness and smug prettiness. Now that she was leaving it she felt a strong wave of affection for the many precious memories it held for her.

Reaching the end of the street, she climbed expertly over a fence and, taking off her sandals, headed through the soft thick grass toward a clump of trees in the distance. In this spot, the brook after which the town had been named swelled into a small lake, its banks skirted by overhanging willows.

She walked toward the oldest and most gnarled of

them, ducking under its veil of softly swinging branches, and sank down into the velvet grass. The tree was Sally's secret wailing wall, wishing well, and fortress all in one. Even as a child, she had hated to make emotional displays before anyone and it was to this tree she had always come with her private joys, sorrows, and dreams.

She remembered with a smile the time she had cried her nine-year-old heart out here when Billy Chandler, her beau of nearly a year, had dropped her for a plump girl with yellow curls. All the little heart-aches and triumphs of childhood had been lived out under the privacy and protection of this gnarled old tree.

From the secure, childish memories her thoughts flew to her future in New York. What a very different world it would be, she sighed. She was extraordinarily lucky and she knew it. To get on a New York paper was the dream of half the journalists in the country. So what was this dread nagging at the back of her mind when she should be filled with nothing but excitement and anticipation?

Absently her long fingers twined round and round a blade of grass. She felt some assurance when she reminded herself that *The Globe* had, after all, used her coverage of the mine disaster instead of sending down one of their own reporters. At least somebody had judged her work good enough for the paper. She knew that most decisions were made directly by Rafe Hawker himself and wondered if he had given his personal approval for her story. She was puzzled by the uncomfortable sensation the thought created.

Sometimes, she thought with impatience, I'm shamefully immature. It's not as if I were an inexperienced teenager going into the terrible big city. Why, most girls my age in Glenbrook already have the responsibility of a family and I'm sitting here indulging myself in fantasies instead of going home to tell the news to Uncle John and Aunt Emily.

With guilty haste she jumped up and, brushing the

fallen leaves from her clothes and hair, she made her way purposefully toward home.

The next two weeks were hectic. Her family took the news with excitement and pride and immediately began to plan a series of farewell parties and dinners in her honor. In a small town like Glenbrook, Sally's good fortune was soon known by everyone, and it became the subject of general discussion.

Only Aunt Emily was less than enthusiastic about her niece's imminent departure. "If you're sure that is what you want, darling . . ." she had said doubtfully when Sally had broken her news. She was far too discreet and understanding to raise objections, but her niece was certain she was taking it much harder than the rest of the family.

Sally's father, a teacher, had died two months before she was born and she lost her mother when she was three. Aunt Emily, her mother's sister with five children of her own, had taken in the little girl without hesitation and lavished on her all the love and concern a mother could. She had never been made to feel like a stepchild; in fact, though Emily had two daughters of her own, it was generally understood that Sally was her favorite.

Her uncle John Holloway, a gentle, quiet man, was the town pharmacist, scrupulously honest and so loath to press his customers for money owed him that there was never much of it in his own home. But the Holloways, managing on laughter, love, and good spirits, were one of the happiest families in town.

Sally's cousins, all older than she, had left home, and even though they still met at their parents' home for dinner at least once a week, Sally felt vaguely as if she were abandoning her aunt and uncle. In the following days of packing and farewells she caught many a wistful glance cast in her direction.

"I won't be so very far away, you know," Sally tried to comfort her aunt. "New York is really only a few hours away."

"That's much too far if you happen to be sick or need us," her aunt said unhappily, then seemed to take a little comfort after extracting the promise from her niece that she would telephone the moment there was anything wrong, and would write long accounts home of her life in the city.

"And we can come up and visit you some weekends and of course you will come home for all the holidays," she added, brightening a little.

Aunt Emily did her best to seem cheerful in the following days, but Sally knew she would have been much happier if she, like most of her girl friends, had chosen a hometown boy and a secure life in Glenbrook rather than the uncertainty and challenge of a career in a big city. Most of these friends had once shared Sally's dreams of making exciting lives for themselves in New York, but one by one they had settled for happy, if uneventful, lives right here in town. Now they looked at her with a little envy as they shared their last days together and helped her choose the clothes and belongings she was taking to the city with her.

Sally had said good-bye to her colleagues on *The Patriot* a week before she was to leave for New York, finishing early so she would have time for last-minute details. There had been yet another party given for her by the staff on her last day there. Smithy, who hated to have it known that he had a soft spot, had to keep disappearing into his office on the pretext of some important business, each time emerging a little more misty eyed. Sally had thought she had taken her last leave of *The Patriot* on that occasion, but now, two nights before her departure, she had a sudden nostalgic urge to see the place once more.

Making a vague excuse to her aunt, she pocketed her office key and slipped out into the warm June night. She had hoped the walk would relax her, but by the time she stepped into the dark old building the apprehension and regret that had filled the last days seemed to overwhelm her. Turning on the lights, she took the stairs to the first floor where the editorial offices were.

She sighed as the happy memories of her more than two years here crowded in on her. She felt her throat constrict with a wistful ache and wandered toward the door of Smithy's office, which opened directly from the reporters' room. Pausing for a moment at the door, she turned on his light and her eyes widened, then misted over at the first thing they encountered.

Directly opposite her, on the wall above Smithy's desk, hung her *Globe* front page, newly framed. Its whiteness and newness stood out from the faded yellow of the collection of old ones. These framed front pages, a feature of newspaper offices everywhere, were milestones in history, in particular of the fifty years Smithy had spent in journalism. They were some of the greatest headlines of his time, announcing everything from a declaration of war to the deaths of Presidents. And among these momentous hallmarks, he had placed her own insignificant front-page story. His gesture of affection and pride made her chin tremble.

No longer bothering to check the tears that were crowding her eyes, Sally stumbled to the old man's desk and, sinking into the leather armchair, buried her head in her arms.

She sobbed with all the emotion that had been pent up in her during the past few days when, outwardly composed, she had been saying good-bye to all that was familiar and loved. She felt release come with her tears and abandoned herself to them completely when, a long while later, an odd sensation made her stop abruptly. An inexplicable chill sent a shudder through her. Fearfully she looked up.

There, leaning against the door, hands deep in his pockets, a man stood regarding her with vague interest. In the instant her eyes traveled to his face, she had taken in that he was exceptionally tall, lean almost on the verge of thinness, but with a powerful masculinity. His hair was dark, his sinewy face made sharp by strong features.

Granite gray eyes held Sally's tear-stained ones. For a moment, unable to move them, she gazed at him helplessly. The man's stare was impersonal, remorseless, sending a burning sensation of embarrassment over her skin.

Frantically, she wondered how long he had been standing there watching her, and the thought made her cringe inwardly. Blood pounded in her ears as she felt a crushing humiliation under the stranger's noncommittal stare. Feeling the burning sensation reach her cheeks, she tore her eyes away from his with a wrenching effort and lowered them defensively behind thick lashes still beaded with tears.

Looking steadfastly at her tightly clenched hands on the desk before her she felt an urgent need to break the strangling silence. "Can I help you?" she stammered in a faint voice, realizing a moment later that it was the most idiotic thing she could have said under the circumstances. She felt a wild urge to run from the room and away from his steady stare but she was unable to lift her eyes, let alone make a move.

Suddenly a long-fingered strong hand thrust a crisply laundered linen handkerchief at her. He had come over to the desk so soundlessly that she was caught unawares and now he stood towering above her.

"I think you had better help yourself first." The voice was quiet, authoritative, and piercingly ironic.

Taking the handkerchief with muttered thanks, she dabbed at her eyes. What now? she wondered with panic as she sat with her head bowed. She had been caught in a mortifying situation by a perfect stranger but that was no reason why she should become practically paralyzed, she tried to reason with herself. She would have to do something to ease this tension at once, give some sort of explanation. But she really had no suitable explanation to offer to this man with the chilling eyes, she thought with fresh alarm. It would only make matters worse.

Mercifully then, the stranger moved away and eased himself into a chair opposite her, thrusting out his long legs before him.

"Do you come here to . . . ah . . . cry often?" he drawled.

The mocking tone in his voice was just the provocation she needed to rally her spirit. "I never cry!" she flared indignantly. "That is, I haven't for years," she stammered, noting with resentment the hint of amusement around his firm mouth.

Again her eyes were locked on his face, this time defiantly, as with a faint frown she withstood his scrutiny. His eyes roamed over her with detachment.

"I work here, at least I did until a few days ago, so I might be able to help with whatever it is you want," she said pointedly, realizing for the first time that the man, whoever he was, had no business being here.

"Were you fired?" he asked, heading off her attempt at a businesslike manner.

"No," she snapped, and this time it was anger that colored her cheeks. "I have another job, on a New York paper, and I'm leaving for it the day after tomorrow." Hope that his questioning would be stopped short by the brusqueness of her manner faded when she saw a frown cross his face.

"Which paper? What job?"

Annoyed at this insolent persistence, when it was surely he who owed her an explanation for being here, she answered him tersely and in a tone that clearly implied it was none of his business, then repeated her own question firmly.

"As you see, it is long past business hours and I should like to close up now," she added challengingly.

"I am waiting for Mr. Smith," he replied after a pause just long enough to be deliberate, and added in his mocking tone, "but don't trouble yourself, he knows I'm here."

There was nothing really lacking in his manners; rather, he was totally arrogant, she decided, realizing that he was not going to give his name or state his business. Shrugging, she headed for the door, eager to make her escape. She didn't really want to know and she wasn't going to ask. The few words they had exchanged had already managed to create considerable friction between them in an incredibly short time and she was not anxious to prolong their acquaintance.

He had strolled over to the wall and stood with his back to her, looking at the framed pages, when he turned abruptly. "Is this yours?" he asked, pointing to her framed front page.

Once more she felt herself pinned by that hard steely gaze but this time she returned it with more boldness than she felt. She was contemptuous of and bitterly regretted her earlier temerity and promised herself not to repeat it again.

He was in his late thirties, she guessed. His tanned face was not typically handsome but very attractive and easily commanded attention. He certainly had hers! Fleetingly she noted the faultless cut of the rather conservative gray wool suit, the immaculate pale gray shirt, the silk burgundy tie. He wore expensive clothes with a careless, easy elegance.

She nodded mutely in reply to his question, feeling the color rise in her cheeks again, and cursed this childish habit of blushing she had not managed to outgrow.

His eyes on her were narrowed, speculative, and her hands moved in a restless, automatic gesture to smooth down the simple cotton dress she was wearing. Her bare tan legs felt uncomfortably exposed. Although she felt his gaze totally disconcerting, she did not withdraw her own but instead drew herself a little straighter and lifted her chin. The unconscious gesture of defiance seemed to amuse him, and he looked at her with a half-smile.

Just then the outer door was thrown open and

Smithy came bustling in. For a moment he stopped in his tracks, looking with astonishment from one to the other.

"Here you are," he burst out, slightly out of breath. "I've been looking for you," he said, and turning to Sally, adding accusingly, "Your Aunt Emily had no idea where you were. I wanted to bring you over at once to introduce you but I see you have already met. Well, Rafe, what do you think of her?"

Long afterward Sally could still vividly remember the physical shock of realization. Clutching at the door frame behind her for support, her eyes shot involuntarily to Rafe Hawker. Of all the people in the world, it had to be him, she thought bitterly as the embarrassing details of the last fifteen minutes flashed before her.

His cold self-assurance and his scorn needed no explanation now. How he must have been filled with contempt for her behavior, especially after he had found out she now worked for him. No wonder he had frowned in disapproval when she had boldly told him that she was going to work on his New York paper. Rafe Hawker, who had a reputation for intolerance of weakness, who did not suffer fools, confronted by a tearful little mess who was crying her eyes out on the eve of going to work on his most important paper. For once, she thought the myth was certainly not larger than the man. He more than lived up to everything she had ever heard about him.

Hawker's answering glance was expressionless. For a moment she was certain he would say in answer to Smithy's question that he had seen enough of her to know she was completely unsuited for a job like that. Instead, he turned to the older man and asked dryly, "And when was Miss Spencer's job on *The Globe* arranged?"

"As I mentioned to you when you phoned this evening, they were very much impressed with her work on that mining story." Smithy explained the situation, greatly embellishing the story with lavish praise of her abilities until Sally closed her eyes in humiliation and prayed fervently that the ground would open under her so she could sink out of sight.

"I have great respect for Mr. Smith's judgment," Hawker said to her coolly when the explanation had been given. And that, she supposed, was to be taken by them as his acceptance. Although his tone was polite and noncommittal, she felt certain he was more than a little displeased with the arrangement.

Turning back to the editor, Hawker continued, "I'm sorry to have sprung my visit on you so unexpectedly. My plane had to stop for refueling in the area so I decided to use your airfield and take the opportunity to finally look over the setup here." Glancing at his watch, he added, "I have less time than I calculated, however, so I will have to get a closer look another time. I'm due to get clearance in a half-hour or so and I have to be in Boston for a meeting later tonight."

Smithy, obviously disappointed that Rafe Hawker, after finally making it to Glenbrook, would not be staying to be shown over the paper, expressed his hopes that they would meet again soon and offered to drive him to the small local airport on the outskirts of town.

"Thank you, but I hired a car at the airport," the publisher declined. Turning to Sally he said, "I'll drop you at your home on my way." It was not a question and did not seem to require acceptance from her. She wondered ruefully if she was in for a lecture once out of Smithy's sight. Anything would be a welcome change from this cold disapproval, she thought with resignation.

The two men talked business for a few minutes more, then, shaking hands, parted. With an almost pleading look at Smithy, Sally waved in farewell. The old man returned the gesture with a meaningful though, Sally thought grimly, completely misplaced wink. She followed the striding figure out of the building.

Once inside the hired limousine, she felt a heart-pounding awareness of his closeness and resisted the temptation to huddle into the far corner of the car. Instead she sat rigidly in the middle of her seat, her eyes directed straight ahead. Apart from the necessary questions and replies regarding which direction he was to take, there was no conversation. Apparently he was not a man to indulge in idle chatter just to put someone at their ease. She wanted frantically to clutch at this chance to explain herself to him, to try to correct his first impression of her.

Sneaking a sideways look at him, she saw his aquiline profile set in grim lines in the faint glow from the dashboard, and felt that any explanation would be hopeless. What could she possibly tell him, anyway? That she was a twenty-four-year-old woman who dissolved into tears at the thought of leaving home for the big city? It would only strengthen his contempt for her. They drove on in silence, Sally forlornly feeling the minutes ticking away, but unable to say anything. Finally the car stopped outside her house.

Turning off the motor, Hawker looked out of the window for a long moment, his eyes wandering over the Holloway home. It was a handsome three-story building with a wide porch circling three sides. Two giant maples stood guard over it in the large front yard, stirring softly in the evening breeze. A light from one of the ground-floor rooms threw a faint yellow glow on her aunt's pretty flower garden. There was a quiet, warm stillness, broken only by the boisterous serenade of crickets. The fragrance of recently cut lawns lingered in the air.

"So this is Aunt Emily's house?" he asked, his glance returning to her. She remembered that Smithy had mentioned her aunt in front of him and she was surprised at his memory and at the faint, almost undetectable bitterness she was sure his voice held. "From what I saw tonight, you seem altogether too reluctant to leave it. I wonder if it is wise for you to do so."

Instantly on the defense, she saw her chance to redeem herself. "Look, Mr. Hawker," she said, trying hard for composure, "I have no doubt disgraced myself in your eyes tonight and I regret, more than you can know, that you saw me cry. No one else has for years, I can assure you. But just because it is my misfortune to have a foolish sentiment about leaving the home and people I have known all my life, it does not follow that I am unworthy of working for *The Globe.* I did not win this job in a school competition, you know!"

Green eyes blazing in the semidarkness, soft lips set firmly, she looked stubbornly at him, feeling a nervous sense of satisfaction at having finally said what she had been holding back for some time.

He looked back at her, obviously amused by her little speech of defiance, his eyes roving over her features, intense and searching. They lingered on her mouth, traveled down her slender throat and back to her wide eyes again.

This time his gaze was not at all impersonal. Her hand, clasped in her lap, began to shake, and she felt the skin on the back of her neck begin to burn. Her breath caught so that she made a little gasping sound. Unbearable as the moment was, she was powerless to break it. She looked at him, mesmerized, forgetting who he was, aware only that he was a man who looked at her like no other ever had and who made her feel sensations that were strange and a little frightening.

It was he who finally broke the trance, leaning away from her and remarking with cool sarcasm, "That sounds like the defense to an attack I haven't made yet . . . Miss Spencer."

Sally felt a sense of total defeat. Without looking at him again, she opened the door and stepped blindly from the car. By the time she got to the gate, he was there holding it open for her. His face was once more cold and expressionless.

"Thank you very much for the lift . . . and goodbye," she said in a barely audible voice, avoiding his eyes.

"See you in New York," he replied lightly, getting into his car.

Standing on the porch, looking after the receding taillights, she said to herself softly, "I hope not. Oh, I sincerely hope not, Mr. Hawker."

CHAPTER TWO

It was the end of Sally's fourth week on *The Globe* and she was still a little unused to the awesome size and breathtaking pace of the paper. The month had seemed like a lifetime in many ways, yet it had gone rapidly.

Looking about at the expense of the room with its multitude of desks, taking up almost an entire floor of the building, she felt a quick pride and satisfaction at being part of it all. With a frown, she remembered her first day on the paper.

When she had walked into the city room that Monday morning a month ago, she had been uneasily aware that the stares directed at her contained more than the usual curiosity afforded a newcomer. Even Bill McIntire, the city editor, had given her a long, too thorough look when she had been introduced to him, and the rest of the staff kept up their barely disguised scrutiny during the next few days.

Sally was puzzled but she did her best to ignore it and set her mind firmly to the tasks assigned her. And what tasks, she sighed now with an impatient grimace. For the past four weeks she had been given nothing an inexperienced cub reporter could not have handled.

Still, she shrugged, she supposed that was quite fair. She *was* a newcomer to one of the country's most powerful newspapers and it was only to be expected that she would be put through a trial. All the same, she couldn't help feeling some frustration. She had come to New York with a determination and drive to do well. So far it hadn't been an illustrious beginning. If she wasn't given a decent story soon, she would have to take matters into her own hands. . . .

It was Mike Costello, the paper's star columnist, who had eventually thrown light on the mystery of the undue curiosity about her.

"I've been watching you with covert adoration these past few days. You look like a freshly picked peach, all dewy and downy," he had said, ambling over to her desk a few days after her arrival and wrapping his arm loosely around her shoulders.

Annoyed at his familiarity, Sally had looked up at him with a frown, changing it to a smile when her eyes met his. He looked too pleasant and good humored to take offense at, she decided.

Introducing himself, his eyes flicked with unconcealed admiration over her slim figure, appraising the crisp linen dress which deepened the green of her eyes and heightened her tan, and over the honey-colored hair that seemed too heavy for her slender neck.

Mike was a strikingly handsome man in his midthirties, with more than his fair share of charm. Dark haired, tall, with a dazzling smile, a swarthy complexion, and vivid blue eyes full of humor, he was the picture of an already successful man determinedly climbing his way closer to the top. Underneath that charm and good humor was a fiercely ambitious, hard-bitten character, Sally was to discover after a short acquaintance. His charm helped him get into the confidence of some very important people and his ambition made the best use of this gift. His firsthand access to influential people made him a good columnist and a valuable asset to the paper.

"You're too damned pretty and totally out of place in this room full of hollow-eyed, unhealthy-looking characters," he said, continuing his intimate banter. "Someone from the art department must have hired you to brighten up this drab place."

"There certainly doesn't seem to be any other use for me," she agreed, a frustrated sigh escaping her. "I do feel a bit useless. This," she said with a depreciating wave at the papers on her desk, "is the sort of stuff I've been assigned all week."

Mike's eyebrows had shot up in surprise as he regarded her a little skeptically. After a speculative pause, he suggested with studied carelessness, "Why don't you complain to him? Say you want something more worthy of your talents?"

"Oh, I couldn't do that," Sally protested hastily, already regretting her complaint. "Mr. McIntire has enough to contend with already without me pestering him. No, I'll just have to—"

"Come on now," Mike cut in with a meaningful grin. "You know I don't mean McIntire." At Sally's puzzled expression his impertinent grin widened. "You know I mean the Hawk."

For a moment she was too confused to do anything but stare at him, her lips parted in amazement. Feeling the color rise in her cheeks at the mention of that name, she collected herself and asked with an incredulous stammer, "What . . . what exactly do you mean?"

Mike's smile was maddeningly indulgent. "Sweetheart, we all know about Hawker."

"Know what?" She felt like screaming at him but managed to keep her voice low.

"Well, that you come with his personal . . . ah . . .

recommendation. That he recruited you himself from what's-its-name, that small Pennsylvania town you come from," he explained, a little less sure of himself now under her stony stare.

Sally continued to gaze at him, unable to speak for a long moment while her mind darted about. Then the full absurdity of what he had been saying dawned on her. "So that's why everyone . . ." The rest of the sentence was lost in a burst of laughter.

It was Mike's turn to stare in amazement now. He looked at the lovely young woman, her head thrown back, one slender hand pressed against her mouth, trying to suppress the rising mirth. His smile flickered uncertainly.

"Sally, you look delicious when you laugh like that, but would you mind letting me in on the joke?" he pleaded.

"Gladly, and I would appreciate it if you let every-one else in on it too," she replied crisply. "The fact is, you could not be more wrong. I do not come with Mr. Hawker's particular, as you call it, recommenda-tion, nor even with his approval, I suspect," adding this last more to herself than him. "I don't know how this rumor could have started but I would be most grateful if you could lay it to rest as soon as possible. Why," she stressed with slight sarcasm, "it makes me feel like an impostor to be the subject of such unde-served fascination. Do you suppose I would be doing this sort of stuff," she pointed with distaste at the papers on her desk, "if I was under his . . . patronage?"

"Maybe reporting isn't what he had in mind for you," he ventured. Instantly seeing the cold look of anger on the girl's face at this brazen hint, he made a hasty apology and at once changed his tactics. "Come to think of it, it wouldn't be at all like the Hawk to pull a stunt like that," he volunteered, trying to appease her. "He would be the last person to plant someone in our midst who he was interested in. He's much too secretive about his private life for that.

Besides," he added with a smirk, "I think his rewards take other forms."

"Well, that at least clears Mr. Hawker's character," Sally replied sarcastically. Her look of distaste for the turn the conversation had taken was not lost on Mike but he made another attempt to get to the bottom of their relationship.

"Journalists are the greatest gossips," he said placatingly. "It goes with the occupation. Naturally, Hawker is our number-one target, being especially fascinating since no one really knows anything about him, except that he is rich, powerful, and pays for our daily bread. He could be the greatest playboy this town has ever seen," he continued with undisguised envy, "but apart from occasionally being seen with some of the world's most beautiful women, he is very unsociable."

Looking at her speculatively, he probed, "How do you suppose the rumor about you two started? Have you actually met him?"

"Yes, once a few weeks ago when he dropped in for a few minutes at the paper where I worked," Sally replied, making an effort to keep her voice impersonal despite the still-disturbing memory of that night. She felt she had had quite enough of this conversation. "The meeting was entirely by accident and lasted only a few minutes." The look she gave Mike convinced him she would say no more on the subject.

Back at her small apartment that night, she had time to go over her conversation with the columnist. How could such a preposterous rumor have started? She wondered uneasily if the phone call Smithy had made recommending her for a job on *The Globe* and dropping Hawker's name as persuasion could have been the cause of it all. It took very little to nurture a vague suspicion into a full-blown bit of gossip on a newspaper. It would certainly explain a great many things.

Bill McIntire's almost hostile attitude was, for instance, one thing that bothered her. The city editor was a brusque man in a continual state of agitation, the burden of running the city desk of the paper clearly evident in his face and temper. He was short with all his reporters but had been particularly morose with Sally. No wonder! If he was under the impression that she had been planted on his staff as a reward for . . . The very thought made her blush violently.

And the rest of the staff! Her mind suddenly darted to Althea Beecham, the frosty blonde beauty who was *The Globe*'s social columnist. One day when they were both waiting for the elevator, she had noticed the blonde woman openly staring at her. This frank scrutiny was all the more surprising because Althea had an unflattering reputation for haughty aloofness, a disdain for the others on the paper's staff.

Sally, who had learned all this from her colleagues, was therefore puzzled when she found herself under the girl's unwavering, cold, and definitely appraising stare. Deliberately, she had looked into the icy blue eyes with a smile and said a cheerful "good afternoon," which the other girl acknowledged with haughty condescension.

She now wondered if Althea's unprecedented interest in another member of the staff had been aroused by the rumors which Sally just found out had been circulating about herself since her arrival. Althea's family, she had heard, was acquainted with Rafe Hawker, and it was quite possible the girl had a personal interest in the millionaire. She certainly qualified as one of those stunningly beautiful women Mike had mentioned in connection with the publisher.

The doorbell interrupted Sally's thoughts and she hurried to answer it. Her callers were Cathy and Margaret, two nurses who shared the apartment below Sally's.

"We've come to tackle the bathroom," Margaret announced, and Sally remembered that the three of them had made plans earlier in the week to repaper her attractive old-fashioned bathroom.

"If you're sure you're not too tired," she said gratefully, getting out the gay floral paper she had purchased a few days before.

"It will be a refreshing change from the kind of drudgery we've been performing all day," Cathy said, grabbing one of the rolls of wallpaper and heading purposefully toward the bathroom. "Besides," she added over her shoulder, "it's only fair that we work for that terrific supper you promised us."

The girls had been acquainted with Sally long enough to appreciate her outstanding abilities in the kitchen, a talent she had inherited from her Aunt Emily. Living on hospital fare as they mostly did, they were always starved for good home cooking, Cathy being especially partial to good food as her round, dimpled figure attested.

Soon the three young women were deep in conversation as they measured, cut, and pasted the paper. Despite all the warnings she had been given about the heartbreaking impersonality of New York, Sally had settled in with ease and speed. She loved the city, and the magic of living there had not yet worn off. She had visited it several times before but living in it was a very different matter.

Part of the reason she had been able to feel at home so soon she attributed to her good fortune in finding such a pleasant little apartment. It was in the East Seventies, close enough to *The Globe* to walk there on fine days. The apartment took up the top floor of a spacious old brownstone in a quiet tree-lined street. The branches of one large tree were just visible from one of the windows, giving her a comforting reminder of home. The apartment was a studio that consisted of one spacious room with a sleeping alcove partitioned off at one end. Although not very high ceilinged, the room had windows on two sides, giving it an airy lightness. There was a tiny kitchen, barely big enough to hold the refrigerator, stove, and sink, and a surprisingly large bathroom with old-fashioned porcelain fittings and an ancient roomy bathtub.

The place had been bare when she had taken it, but now, a month later, it was transformed into a stylish little home with imaginative rather than expensive furniture. Most of the pieces were either wicker or wrought iron to give the room a more spacious look. A profusion of potted plants, brightly colored rugs from an Indian bazaar, cherished odds and ends, and favorite books and family photographs from her own room in Glenbrook lent the place an air of comfort and gaiety.

"You've really done wonders with this place." Cathy looked around with admiration when their papering was done. They were sitting at the wrought iron and glass table, awaiting the meal Sally had prepared.

"You should have seen what a mess it was in when the last tenant—a bachelor *and* an artist—lived here," Margaret said. "Still, we should cast no stones; it took Cath and me almost a year to get beyond the mattress-on-the-bare-floor stage."

"Yes, Sally," Cathy sighed in agreement, "you're the kind of girl I always meant to be but never quite had the energy to turn into. Here you are, only a few weeks in New York, and you already seem to have everything under control."

Not quite, Sally thought to herself wryly, but she smiled at the compliment. It was true that, thanks to Aunt Emily's gentle insistence, she had become an expert cook and a conscientious housekeeper while still a teenager. The delicious smells that emanated from her tiny kitchen were quite atypical of a bachelor apartment. Although she was a light eater, whatever she prepared was done with habitual care. She could no more eat out of a carton from the refrigerator than she could leave a sink full of dirty dishes overnight.

"There's just one more thing this apartment needs," Cathy said with a mischievous grin. When the other two looked at her questioningly she blurted out triumphantly, "A man!"

"And speaking of the species," Margaret put in, "Cathy and I just happened to have our eyes glued to the keyhole the other night when a certain dark, extremely handsome gentleman escorted you home. Is he someone special or is it too impertinent to ask?"

"Not at all," Sally laughed. "That's Mike Costello, a columnist on *The Globe*. If you find him all that fascinating I'd be only too happy to share him with you. He has more than enough charm to go around for the three of us, I can assure you. Why don't I invite him to dinner here one night and then you girls can see him eye to eye instead of through the keyhole?"

The girls greeted the proposal with unanimous enthusiasm, and after chatting for a while longer they got up to leave, pleading early-morning calls at the hospital where they worked.

Sally had become fond of the two of them. They had become friends as soon as they met when she moved into the building. And inviting Mike to dine here in their company was a stroke of genius for which she congratulated herself.

It was time she invited him, since he had already taken her out several times, but she knew she would be more comfortable if she were not left entirely alone with him. Despite the fact that she could see straight through his too obvious and deliberate charm and the motivation behind it, she could not help liking him.

Sally had the feeling Mike was not altogether convinced by her explanation regarding Hawker. He often dropped the publisher's name into the conversation, watching covertly for her reaction. She always refused the bait and changed the subject as soon as she could, much to his dissatisfaction. Mike was successful with any woman he decided to captivate, and he set out with equal dedication to turn the head of a switchboard girl or the wife of a prominent politician. When he noticed that Sally was not susceptible to his charms and laughed at his attempts at seduction as often as not, he took it as a challenge and became more and more persistent and earnest in his pursuit of her.

When his dazzling smiles and heady compliments left her unmoved, he tried to impress her with his important connections. He had already taken her to dinner at Sardi's, to lunch at 21 and other favorite celebrity haunts where he seemed to be on a familiar basis with everyone.

Sometimes she became annoyed at his persevering attentions, but on the whole she enjoyed his company. When he wasn't trying so hard, he was excellent company. He had a great sense of humor which in rare moments of honesty he would turn against himself with skilled self-mockery. Mike was brazen but usually stopped just short of being objectionable so there was little awkwardness between them. At the end of the evenings when he brought her home, Sally would laugh off his romantic advances and he would usually end up laughing along resignedly.

One night on their way home in a cab he turned to her in mock despair. "After very careful deliberation through many sleepless nights, I've arrived at the conclusion that you must have a very big fish hooked, waiting to be reeled in, to be able to withstand my own, I'm told not inconsiderable, charm."

"After very little deliberation at all, I have come to the conclusion that you are far too meek and modest, and if you keep wallowing in your present state of humility, you are in danger of becoming a pitiful introvert," she teased back, hoping to head off the obvious turn the conversation was taking.

"You have done your utmost to sabotage my self-confidence, you must admit that," he complained. "Tell me honestly, though, has there ever been a man to make your unmelting little heart flutter?"

"Certainly," she replied. "There was Billy Chandler, but he threw me over for a blonde," she said with a straight face but laughing inwardly as she remembered her broken affair in the fourth grade.

Detecting a michievous glint in her eyes, Mike persisted, "You must admit your air of mystery does arouse some rather obvious suspicions."

Sally tensed. Why must he keep needling her like this?

Sitting by her open window that night, Sally's thoughts drifted to the man she had tried unsuccessfully to close out of her mind. Now that she was working in the same building and living in the same city as Rafe Hawker, he seemed more remote than ever. She had not seen him again since that first ignominious meeting in Glenbrook a few weeks earlier, and though she tried not to think of either him or their meeting, his name was on the lips of the other reporters so often that she could not avoid it.

It appeared she was one of a very few on the staff who had actually had a conversation, no matter how brief, with him. The others occasionally saw him stride through the editorial office to exchange a few words with Bill McIntire, but he rarely acknowledged the presence of anyone else and he had an aloofness which completely discouraged familiarity. He was never known to lose his temper with anyone, but his cold, sarcastic contempt for anyone who failed to do his job properly made him seem more menacing than if he had been given to violent outbursts and he inspired a universal respect.

His decisions penetrated every department, yet his penthouse office, the seat of his power, was a world remote from the rest of the paper. Sally tried to shake his oppressive presence from her mind with the comforting thought that, like her colleagues, she could probably work on *The Globe* for years to come without ever crossing his path again.

The following Monday morning Sally finally had the break she had been waiting for. She was sent out on what promised to be a commonplace enough story, to interview an elderly woman who was being forcibly evicted from the home she had lived in for more than forty years. The old building in Brooklyn in which she lived was being torn down to make room for a business complex. The old woman, with a lifetime of memories binding her to it, refused to budge from the place, and stubbornly continued to barricade herself in, long after the other tenants had left. Running out of methods of persuasion and patience, the developers had finally turned to the police.

The story was a daily occurrence in New York, where thousands of people were uprooted every year in the relentless path of progress. But in the small town from where Sally came things like this did not happen, and she was deeply moved by the old lady's plight. She went back to the office, the light of determination in her eyes, her small mouth set firmly, to write her story.

Words flooded from her typewriter in a bitter indictment of the heartlessness of a city that was so bent on growth that it trampled underfoot the very people who had made it great. A half hour after handing in her story, she was summoned by one of the senior editors. He looked at her with a searching frown for a long moment.

"I was not aware we had assigned you to write an editorial," he said gruffly, with a short pause during which Sally's heart sank. "But this stuff is not bad. Reminds me of those heartbreak stories O. Henry used to write about this city. We'll use it on page three tomorrow."

Sally floated back to her desk. She was certain there could be no satisfaction equal to that of having done a good job on a story. Journalism, despite its many corruptions, was a noble profession after all: crusading, informative, and entertaining all at the same time. It was worth waiting a whole frustrating month for even that offhand praise, "not bad."

The rest of the day passed quickly in the completion of other tasks. As she was ready to leave, Mike ambled up to her.

"That becoming flush on your cheeks and that sparkle in your eyes, are they caused by my approach?" he asked hopefully.

"As a matter of fact, no. They are caused by one of the senior editors," she replied enigmatically.

"Which one?" he demanded, looking about the room, and she had to laugh at the indignant look on his face. She told him then about her story, and he seemed genuinely pleased for her.

Sitting down on the edge of her desk, he proposed, "That definitely calls for the biggest celebration this town has ever seen. Will you have dinner with me tonight?"

"I was thinking it was high time I reciprocated and cooked you a meal," she told him. "Two of my neighbors, girls who share the apartment below mine, are very anxious to meet you, if you would care to come to dinner tonight."

A look of disappointment crossed Mike's face at the mention of the two girls, and he made it clear that he was not pleased with the idea of having chaperones. But he accepted the invitation with pleasure and taking one of her hands into his, he gazed deeply into her eyes. Parodying his best seductive manner he murmured, "You mean these fair and tender hands are going to prepare a meal for me?"

Laughingly, she tried to pull away, but he held her hand firmly and raised it to his lips.

A tall figure stopped in midstride by her desk at that instant. Rafe Hawker, taking in the scene with one swift look, briefly and contemptuously glanced at Mike. The coldly penetrating look he let linger on Sally drained her face of color.

CHAPTER THREE

The look Hawker had given her stayed with Sally like a chilling omen. Thinking about it that night while preparing dinner for her guests, she was filled with uneasiness that went beyond the embarrassment of the moment.

She pushed back a lock of hair with exasperation as she recalled that twice now in as many meetings he had caught her in a situation where she must have appeared childish and immature. The first time she had been dissolved in tears, and this time, even worse, she had been in the middle of what must have looked to him like a silly, flirtatious tussle with Mike, right there in the city room. Shame washed over her anew and she flushed hotly at the memory.

Still, Hawker's look had contained much more than just the disapproval the situation had warranted. It had held something akin to hostility and something more besides—something she could not name but which filled her with a strange premonition of she wasn't certain what.

The look had obviously not been lost on Mike Costello either, she realized now with dismay. He had looked at her with intense curiosity, his suspicions fanned to a new life. Had he too noticed that the publisher's stare had held hostility? She had not waited to find out and fled the office before Mike could raise the matter.

But he was coming to dinner tonight and she was already thinking with apprehension about the inevitable questions. She was busy turning over plans for fielding them in the best possible way when the doorbell rang. It was too early for any of her guests and she went to the door a little impatiently.

Annoyed, she saw it was Mike. "You're at least a half-hour early. I told you eight o'clock," she said a little ungraciously.

"Really?" he asked innocently. "Well, don't be cross with me, gorgeous. I've been walking around the block for an hour as it is, trying not to seem too eager. Mmm . . . what a heavenly smell!" He sniffed the air, edging his way past her into the room.

Sally saw through the all-too-apparent reason why Mike had come so early. But if he had planned to interrogate her before the other guests arrived, he would be in for a disappointment, she decided.

Accepting the bouquet of roses and the two bottles of chilled, ostentatiously expensive champagne he held out to her, she invited, "Fix yourself a drink and make yourself comfortable while I finish up in the kitchen. The others should be here shortly."

For once she was glad her kitchen was too tiny to admit company. While she was in there busying herself, conversation would be impossible. She would make sure she prolonged her preparations until the two girls from downstairs arrived.

Unnecessarily she fussed with an already perfect meal. She checked the golden crepes stuffed with mushrooms in a savory sour cream sauce that she would be serving for appetizers, lifted the lid on the fragrant, mildly seasoned lamb dish, and took another peek at the apricot mousse dessert in the refrigerator.

She had not long to wait for Margaret and Cathy to arrive. They must have spotted Mike on his way up and followed him shortly. The girls, both in their mid-twenties, were pretty and vivacious enough to inspire Mike to turn on the full force of his charm at once. They were suitably impressed by the handsome, entertaining columnist and he was in his glory, in the midst of such an appreciative audience.

Conversation and laughter were soon flowing freely and Sally, despite her secret preoccupation, found herself enjoying the evening. The dinner was an enormous success, each course being greeted with ecstatic praise from all three guests. Cooking was one of Sally's few vanities and she was gratified by their genuine enjoyment of every mouthful.

The rest of the evening passed in high good humor and it was past midnight when Cathy and Margaret took their leave. Mike, of course, made an excuse to linger behind, just as Sally knew he would.

Closing the door on the departing girls, she sank into an armchair, stretching and closing her eyes in a gesture she hoped would convey her weariness to Mike. Inside, she was tensed for the question she knew would be coming.

After a short pause it did come, blatantly.

"Being a connoisseur of the best things in life, Hawker must really appreciate your excellent cooking," Mike commented with hardly veiled sarcasm.

Now that the attack had come, Sally was surprised at how clumsily it had been delivered. Really she expected a little more skill and finesse from someone like Mike. Her eyes widened and held his for a moment.

With a resigned sigh, she said wearily, "I don't particularly want to hear it, but I suppose you are going to give an explanation for that remark?"

"Come now, surely it's time for you to supply some explanation."

Surprised at the unexpected anger in his voice, Sally shook her head, trying to keep her voice reasonable. "I honestly don't know what you are talking about."

"Don't you really?" he snapped back. "Have you forgotten that I was there this afternoon? Sweetheart, my hair was practically standing on end from the charge of electricity that passed between you and Hawker. The man has never yet noticed the rest of us are alive. Are you going to tell me that high-voltage look he gave you was just a passing glance for one of his staff?"

No, Sally thought, I'm not going to tell you that because I don't know what it was.

Aloud, still with controlled patience, she said, "I expect Mr. Hawker was annoyed at seeing members of his staff cavorting around during working hours. I don't blame him for that and I much rather he had distinguished you with that unpleasant look than me."

"So," Mike's voice rose in anger, "you still insist on going on with this coy little act of yours. For weeks now you have tried to make me believe that there was nothing between you and the almighty Mr. Hawker, that your coming to work at *The Globe* so soon after he paid his little visit to your hometown was just a coincidence. Now do you still expect me to believe all that after that fascinating and sizzling look that I saw him—"

"No, I don't expect you to believe that or anything else!" Sally exclaimed, jumping to her feet. Fists clenched at her sides and green eyes flaming, she faced him. "It doesn't matter in the least what you or anyone else believes. I'm tired of having to justify myself day after day. I have told you the truth over and over again; if you don't choose to believe it, I don't care. This has gone far beyond a joke and I'm thoroughly fed up with your insinuations. How dare you demand explanations from me, anyway? I don't owe you one and from now on you are not getting one. If you won't stop asking me your impertinent questions, we had just better stop seeing each other."

"I'm sorry, Sally," he apologized, much subdued. "I didn't mean to attack you like that. It's just that . . . well, I care for you, I care for you very much, more than I ever have for any girl, and I guess I am suffering from a touch of jealousy and insecurity about where I stand with you."

How many women had longed to hear that declaration from Mike Costello? she wondered fleetingly. Yet to her, the expression of these sentiments was quite unwelcome. Despite his earnest, almost melodramatic manner, she had more than a small doubt about his sincerity. Sally was aware that Mike was attracted to her, but then he seemed to be attracted to almost any reasonably attractive woman. What made her especially desirable to him was the possibility that she was involved with another man—specifically, Rafe Hawker. Realizing this, she could act with less embarrassment and more indifference than had it been anyone but Mike.

"Coveting your neighbor's, or in this case your employer's, goods seems to me to be the case, Mike," she said deprecatingly.

"Granted, I deserve that," Mike conceded placatingly. "But seriously, you must know how I feel about you, how I've felt about you ever since we met."

"Yes, I have a pretty good idea," she agreed with a mocking laugh. "If I had been in any doubt of it I was certainly reassured by that pretty speech you made a while ago."

She noted an almost imperceptible tension cross his face. Mike Costello was not used to rejection and this was certainly shaping up to be one. For a moment his vanity struggled with his purpose. He forced a smile and continued humbly.

"I hope you aren't going to hold that against me. I hope we have become far too good friends for that."

"No, I won't hold it against you," she replied, "only I don't ever want us quarreling on this subject again." Then she added firmly, "Now I really would like to call it a night, Mike. I'm exhausted."

Without further protest Mike took his leave, pausing only to plant a kiss on Sally's reluctantly offered cheek. Closing the door behind him, she leaned against it

tiredly and pushed the hair back from her forehead
in a gesture of utter weariness.

The next morning Sally took her place at her desk
with more than her usual determination to work hard.
She made a deliberate attempt to avoid conversation
with Mike, only briefly returning his greeting, and
spent the whole day fully absorbed in her work. That
was how it would be from now on.

The following day the city editor summoned her to
his office. "This may or may not turn out to be a
good story," Bill McIntire told her. "We've had a tip
that Michelle Campbell-Jones has returned from Europe and is staying at a small West Side hotel. Now I
don't know if it actually is the Campbell-Jones woman,
you'll have to find that out. But if it is, there's bound
to be a good story in the fact that one of America's
richest heiresses has returned in considerable secrecy
from Europe, where she was just supposed to have
gotten herself engaged to a prince—and now she's
hiding out in a nondescript little hotel instead of one
of the luxury ones her parents own."

Sally had mixed feelings about the assignment. She
was surprised and gratified that the city editor had
personally assigned her to a story which could turn
out to be a valuable one for the paper; she must be
going up in his esteem. On the other hand, she was
filled with distaste for the nature of the job.

Snooping around, trying to dig up secrets in prominent people's private lives, was one of the most unpleasant aspects of her profession. Ah, well, you had
to take the bad with the good, she shrugged, making
her way to the photographic department to pick up
Sam Allen, the young photographer who was to accompany her on the story.

The small West Side hotel was neat but had evi-
dently seen much better days. It had an air of shabby
elegance about it. Sally decided to sit in the lobby
while she planned the most discreet way to go about

her inquiries. The place had an atmosphere of refinement about it, not at all conducive to her spying on one of its patrons.

As she sat turning the matter over in her mind she was suddenly alerted by the young photographer beside her. Sam was staring toward the back of the lobby with the intensity of a hunting dog who has spotted its prey. She turned quickly to follow his gaze.

Crossing over from the dining room toward the elevators was a strikingly handsome couple. The girl was dark and slender, the man a perfect contrast of fairness with an athletically built body.

"That's her! That's the Jones dame," Sam hissed excitedly.

By then Sally had also recognized the young woman. She was about her own age, a reputed beauty and justly so, she thought with fleeting admiration. She carried herself with inbred grace as if eternally posing for a portrait, head held regally high, shoulders erect. Even in the dim light her pale skin glowed and her hair glistened darkly.

Sally put a restraining hand on Sam's arm and waited for the couple to get into the elevator. It had an old-fashioned brass indicator above the door and she watched for the floor where it stopped. It stopped at five.

"They shouldn't be hard to find; they were the only couple to get into the elevator, and in a small hotel like this there aren't many rooms on one floor," she told the photographer quietly. "I think I had better go it alone for a while, Sam. If she sees your cameras she might just panic. I'll probably have a better chance if I go up and try to talk to her by myself. I'll call you if I need you."

"Boy, she sure is some looker," Sam whistled in admiration, adding gallantly, "though you're much more my type. Anyway, I've already hung one on her while she was getting into the elevator. I don't know how it will turn out because I took it with this miniature camera, and I didn't dare use the flash, but it'll be better than nothing."

Sally walked to the elevators with all the assurance of someone who had every right to be there. She pressed the button for five and the machine silently ascended to that floor. Once out of the elevator, she immediately sighted the couple standing a few doors away, deep in conversation. Sally fought down her feeling of distaste and walked toward them.

"Miss Campbell-Jones?" she said softly.

The words had a jolting effect on the girl. She looked around in alarm, her eyes instantly darting to her companion. So near, she was even more beautiful than in her many photographs, though her face was marred now by a look of fear.

Sally sensed more than saw her blond companion stiffen, and her eyes traveled to him. Her heart skipped a beat as she recognized Marc Whitfield, the young, glamorous, dynamic senator who was the most popular politician in Washington—and who also happened to be married.

Both she and Sam had been so engrossed in spotting the glamorous heiress that they hadn't even noticed who her secret companion was. Instantly professional, Sally grasped the magnitude of the story.

She could sense Whitfield physically brace himself to face her. "What can we do for you?" he asked courteously, as if she had just gone to his office to ask for his help in something instead of having caught him in a compromising situation. She had to admire his composure under pressure.

"I'm afraid I'm a reporter," Sally divulged frankly. She could see the dark girl shrink back but the senator gave her an almost imperceptible caress of reassurance and took the doorkey from her.

Opening the door, he said with undiminished courtesy, "Shall we go inside?" Miss Campbell-Jones hesitated for a moment, but with another reassuring look from him, she stepped in. The look had clearly said,

"Don't worry, I'll handle this." Sally followed and heard the door close behind her.

They were in the small salon of what was obviously once one of the hotel's luxury suites.

"May I offer you a drink?" Whitfield invited. When both Sally and the heiress declined, he poured one for himself.

"I could, of course, try to give some ambiguous explanation as to why you're seeing us together, but I realize it would still look bad in the press," he began, and Sally again admired his polish in a difficult situation. The woman said nothing, just stared at the white hands clasped in her lap.

"I think I had better tell you the truth, and trust in your discretion and sense of fair play," he continued. "Michelle and I have known each other for almost two years. She went abroad because of me—because of my marriage. We both thought at the time that it would be the decent thing to do." He allowed himself a bitter laugh. "It was a great mistake, one we have both been paying for all this time. The situation is this: I have managed to persuade my wife to give me a quiet divorce, but the moment she finds out about Michelle, all that comes to nothing. A story at this time could ruin our chances of ever getting together. And it won't be long before the divorce comes through."

"A story now would also ruin Marc's career." The girl spoke for the first time. Her eyes were brimming with tears and her low voice was an appeal. Despite her poise and beauty, she looked vulnerably young at that moment.

"I thought you were all set to marry a European prince," Sally cut in in surprise.

"My parents did their best to make that come about but I couldn't, I just couldn't," she said, her voice choking and her eyes turning to the man beside her. A wave of unspoken sympathy passed between the two women. Michelle Campbell-Jones was not a rich heiress then; she was a girl miserably and hopelessly in love.

"I realize that you still have your job to do," Whitfield said matter-of-factly. "But if you could possibly find a way around this, we would give you our promise that in the future when . . . ah . . . our relationship is less vulnerable and ready to be made public, you will have all the exclusive interviews you want. And I, in my political capacity, would always be ready to talk to you."

Sally looked from the handsome young man to the beautiful woman, and what she encountered in that face made up her mind. "I was sent here to interview Miss Campbell-Jones about her reasons for returning from Europe so suddenly. As long as I can do that, I suppose I need not involve you, Senator. If I get my original story, I should still be doing my job."

She cut short their expressions of gratitude. "As far as I know, no one else is aware that either of you is in this hotel. *The Globe* got the tip on Miss Campbell-Jones exclusively. But you're taking an awful chance being together like this. If my advice is of any value, you had better be much more careful in the future, or at least until you are free to be seen in public together."

"Oh, we will," the girl agreed eagerly. "It was just this once because we hadn't seen each other for so long. Marc flew in this morning to have breakfast with me. He is going back to Washington now."

"I'm going down to the lobby to get my photographer. I guess it would be better if you were not here by the time we got back," Sally pointed out to Whitfield. Receiving his firm handshake at the door, she added with a smile, "And don't think me a softy, Senator. I shall hold you to all those Washington scoops you promised me," she told him with a friendly grin.

By the time she returned with Sam Allen, Michelle Campbell-Jones was sitting alone, outwardly composed, in a high-backed chair, looking exactly like someone who broke off engagements to European princes as a matter of course. Only a glance, full of gratitude, in Sally's direction, revealed the secret bond between the two.

Sally got exactly the sort of story *The Globe* rejoiced in, a firsthand interview with a usually unapproachable society figure, including the story of her broken romance. Her conscience was clear; she had not really cheated her paper of a good story. Furthermore, she had the satisfaction of feeling that she had made a friend in Michelle Campbell-Jones and a valuable newspaper contact in Senator Whitfield.

Bill McIntire was pleased with the interview and went as far as showing enthusiasm for something that would make an excellent front page for *The Globe* the following day. It was not the sort of story Sally could take personal pride in, but she was nevertheless satisfied that she had scored another front page in the paper and had pleased the city editor.

 The next day, after the first edition had already hit the streets, a copyboy hurried to her desk. "Mr. McIntire wants to see you at once."

"Come in and close the door," the city editor called out in answer to her knock. His expression was even more grim than usual as he slammed down a photograph in front of her and barked, "Have a look at this."

Sally bent close to the photo and caught her breath at what she saw. It was a dim but still discernible picture of Michelle Campbell-Jones, and at her side, unmistakably, Senator Marc Whitfield. "I hung one on her while she was getting into the elevator." Sam Allen's words came back to her. It was the photograph he had taken so furtively and was not sure would come out. Well, it had come out all right! How could she have been so negligent, how could she have forgotten about it, she cursed herself silently.

"That happens to be Senator Marc Whitfield, probably the best-known face in Washington next to the President," the city editor hissed in fury. "Don't tell me the man was right under your very nose, obviously involved in some sort of hanky-panky with this girl, and you didn't even recognize him?" he thundered.

Sally took a deep breath and without hesitation replied quietly, "Yes, I recognized him."

For a moment Bill McIntire gaped at her in silent astonishment.

"What the hell does that mean?" he bellowed, jumping to his feet and advancing toward her menacingly.

It did not for a moment occur to Sally to lie or give excuses; she told him the whole story. Stunned into silence, the city editor stared at her and occasionally shook his head, as if the impossibility of all he was hearing was too much for him.

"So you took it on yourself to decide what *The Globe* should and should not print," he said after a moment, with a quiet sarcasm that was more ominous than his yelling had been, "and now we've missed out on a fantastic story because *you* chose not to pursue it. Not only have you been grossly negligent in letting a sensational scoop like this escape you, but you have also been unbelievably impertinent. I'm sure our publisher will be delighted to hear that we have hired ourselves not a reporter but a moral conscience in the person of one Miss Sally Spencer."

Any further desire in Sally to fight the issue gave way that instant. The very mention of Rafe Hawker filled her with trepidation; she could think of nothing to say. Here it was, strike three against her in Hawker's book. She left the room without another word.

She realized now only too well that from the paper's point of view she had committed a cardinal sin. But on her own account she could feel no guilt. She got the story she had been sent out to get, though she had let a much better one slip by. Still, the facts she had suppressed were not of national importance or significance. She had cheated no one out of vital information, only of some gossip, the consequences of which could ruin two perfectly decent people's lives.

If city editors and publishers thought that was an essential part of journalism, then they were wrong. She was prepared to fight anyone on that principle. Anyone at all, she promised herself grimly.

Early next morning Bill McIntire summoned her to his office once more. He looked more subdued than on the previous day, even a little uncomfortable, she thought.

"I'm sorry, Sally, but I have instructions to let you go." He broke the news to her bluntly. "I say I'm sorry and I mean it, because you looked like you were becoming a very capable reporter. But damn it, girl," he said with anger flaring afresh, "you can't get away with things like this on a newspaper!"

"Do you mean I'm fired?" asked Sally in a small voice. "For this one incident, in which I still happen to think I was right?"

The city editor nodded without arguing the point. "Yes, those are my instructions. It's not something that I can fight." From his tone Sally detected that he had in fact tried to fight the decision and for this at least she was grateful.

"I guess there's no need for me to ask whether it was Mr. Hawker who 'instructed' you," she sighed.

"It was," Bill McIntire agreed, not raising his eyes to hers.

Sally deliberated for a moment, then drawing her brows in a firm line and lifting her small chin, she declared, "I understand that you can't fight him. But I will!"

The city editor gave her a glance that contained a hint of admiration, then shook his head and said in an almost fatherly tone, "Come on, Sally, save yourself the trouble. No one does that."

"You mean no one has ever stormed those sacred chambers on the twenty-fifth floor and confronted the mighty Mr. Hawker? Even when they thought they were right?"

"No one has," he shrugged. "His decisions have always been final!"

"Then *I* will be the first," she announced stubbornly. "I could never respect myself again if I was so cowed by someone that I didn't stand up for myself."

She left the office and Bill McIntire looked after the determined figure in amazement.

Not allowing herself even a moment's hesitation, Sally marched directly to the elevators and pressed the "up" button. She had been far too easily spellbound and awestruck by the distinguished Mr. Hawker ever since she'd first met the man. She had blushed and paled before his cold and superior presence. Why, she had allowed herself to become as impressed as those silly little office girls she had overheard whispering dreamily about him as if he were some highly desirable romantic idol.

But not anymore! Her job, her career, all her dreams of New York depended on this. She would not let him destroy all that without so much as a whimper.

Not even when she stepped out on the twenty-fifth floor did her spirits flag. She looked about her in the vast marble reception lobby, quiet as a tomb, and wondered which of the doors to take. She had come in such a hurry that she had neither made an appointment nor had asked how to go about seeing him.

Squaring her shoulders, she approached one of the massive doors and when she heard the faint click of typing from within she decided to try there. It was a large reception room, luxuriously furnished. Two immaculately groomed secretaries sat at large desks separated from each other by a sea of plush, emerald-green carpet.

"Can I help you?" one of them inquired softly. Sally supposed voices were never raised above a polite hush in this luxurious sanctuary.

"I would like to see Mr. Hawker," she answered directly.

The girl hesitated just long enough to get across the message that this was not the correct way to go about it, and asked politely, "Have you an appointment?"

"No."

Again a pause during which the two secretaries exchanged glances, and Sally, if she hadn't been so preoccupied, would have enjoyed the silent pantomine of disapproval.

"Just one moment, please," the first girl said. "Would you take a seat?" Sally did so while the secretary disappeared through another large door into an inner office.

A minute later she reappeared. "Would you come this way, please?" Sally followed her into the other room. This was almost as large as the outer one but had a much cozier look about it. There were the same expensive furnishings, deep carpets, and heavy drapes, but there were also a few homey touches—plants, photographs, and a general air of busy untidiness about the large desk where a pleasant-faced, plump, middle-aged woman sat. She looked up at Sally with a friendly smile.

"I understand you would like to see Mr. Hawker?"

"Yes, please, though I don't have an appointment," Sally replied.

"I'm Eve Tarrant, his secretary. I'm afraid I'll have to ask you on what business you would like to see Mr. Hawker."

"He fired me," Sally told her frankly. "I would like to have a few words with him about it."

The woman's eyebrows shot up in surprise, then her face broke into an approving smile.

"I should think you would, and I'm delighted to hear it. Good luck to you," she said with a heartiness that took Sally a little by surprise. It was almost as if she had somehow brightened the woman's day by her announcement. The secretary went to a door on the far side of her office and knocked briskly. Without waiting for a reply, she went in and closed the door behind her.

Sally's courage, which had been flying high until this moment, was about to take a dive with the knowledge that Rafe Hawker was on the other side of that door. He probably would refuse to see her.

Before she had time to take comfort from that thought, the door opened again and the woman, still smiling, beckoned to her.

"Mr. Hawker will see you now."

As Sally walked past her, she thought the woman gave her shoulder a brief, encouraging pat.

CHAPTER FOUR

The room was of generous proportions, an anachronism in the ultramodern Globe Building. Soft light filtered through tall, narrow windows, reflecting off the gleaming mahogany paneling. Oriental rugs were scattered on the highly polished floor and carved bookcases held handsomely bound volumes. There were bronze and marble ornaments everywhere, and oil paintings covered much of the walls.

All this Sally saw only fleetingly, for opposite her, behind a large Empire desk, sat Rafe Hawker. Her resolution almost gave way to familiar tension under his direct, noncommittal stare.

Determined not to be intimidated by it, she said in

a crisp, businesslike manner, "Good morning, Mr. Hawker."

The publisher rose laconically from his desk and indicated a chair nearby. "Won't you take a seat, Miss Spencer?"

Please, please don't let me make a fool of myself in front of him this once, she prayed silently as she took the proffered chair. It was so easy to become unnerved under that penetrating stare. Bracing herself, she began, "You know why I'm here."

"Yes, but I want you to tell me about it." He was leaning back in his chair now, looking at her with a frown of expectation, his voice challenging.

Slowly, she felt the nerves she had tried to keep under control uncoiling inside her. She clenched her hands in her lap and forced her voice to sound even and steady.

"Very well. You have fired me, I think quite unjustly."

"Do go on," he invited with exaggerated politeness.

He was forcing her to be defensive, a position she hated. "I have worked hard and conscientiously since I joined this paper. I did the particular job I was assigned two days ago with equal conscientiousness."

Seeing his eyebrows shoot up at this claim, she repeated with emphasis, "Yes, with good conscience, Mr. Hawker. I completed the story I was assigned. It was a good one, too, as far as this paper is concerned, and it gave *The Globe* its front page yesterday. Anything I left out I believe was indeed a matter of conscience. The information I withheld would have ruined two people's private lives, not to mention the career of one of them. It would have been unneccessary, unfeeling, and unethical."

There was a silence during which Hawker allowed himself a sardonic smile.

"Since you are so well qualified in deciding what is ethical and what is not, since your sense of justice and your conscience are so much more noble than anyone else's on this paper, it seems I had better dismiss Bill McIntire, all the editors, and all your seniors, and let you run *The Globe* single-handedly," he told her coldly.

"Your sarcasm is a very unfair weapon under the circumstances," she cried out. "I'm here fighting for my job, Mr. Hawker, though that might be an insignificant matter to you."

"In that case, don't presume to tell me so righteously where conscience fits into my newspaper. If I still have to explain to you that any well-known person is fair game for public curiosity and that we are in the business to satisfy that curiosity, then I am wasting my time and yours, since you obviously know nothing about journalism."

"I *do* know about journalism. I have learned about it firsthand from a great man who has given fifty years of his life to it," she answered heatedly. "But I won't be convinced that ruining people's lives for the sake of some juicy gossip is a necessary function of the profession."

"In that case you don't know what this particular newspaper is about and you have made a big mistake in joining it. If you spent less time under the spell of our resident Lothario, you might have been able to learn a few essential facts about the paper you work for."

The reference to Mike Costello was unmistakable and Hawker's voice was brittle with resentment. Yet there was no reply she could make because she felt him to be in the right at least on this count. She herself believed that regrettable incident with Mike in the city room was inexcusable, even though she had been an unwilling party to it. She sat motionless, with eyes averted.

"I see you have no reply to that," Hawker pursued. "Every female on the staff has had a bad dose of the Mike Costello epidemic. I could hardly expect you to be immune."

Sally's attention was riveted by the sudden bitterness in his voice. Meeting her gaze he gave her a cynical smile. "Still, I believe Mr. Costello may have met his match at last."

This last remark held a controlled savagery which took Sally completely by surprise. Somehow the conversation had taken an unnerving turn which was making it hard for her to keep her composure. She grasped for an explanation.

"I came up here to see you about my job. I don't see what any of this has to do—"

"Then allow me to enlighten you, starting with the allusion to our esteemed columnist," he interrupted curtly. "When I say I believe he has at last met his match, I mean in unscrupulous ambition. Costello uses anyone he can to further his climb." He paused for a moment and added bitterly, "Just as you have used me, my dear Miss Spencer."

The words had the sting of a powerful slap and Sally felt herself reeling under their impact. She experienced a sickening sensation in the pit of her stomach and it was a while before she had the strength to cry out, "For God's sake, what are you saying to me?"

Unmoved by the confusion and appeal in her voice, he sneered. "If you insist on having it spelled out, though I had expected a little more discretion from you, I will. In short, things have a way of getting back to me."

"Such as?" Her voice was almost inaudible.

"Such as you have somehow managed to lead the entire staff into the impression that you are on this paper as a reward for certain, how shall I say—favors —you have granted me. My mistress, I believe is the quaint, old-fashioned phrase for it."

Ignoring her surprise, he continued with brutal bluntness. "I must say you are an exceptionally imaginative and powerful storyteller if you have managed to blow a small meeting into a passionate liaison. Ordinarily I would be most flattered to be the subject of your fantasies, but I happen to be very particular about my private life. I don't relish real or imaginary stories spread about it." He sat back to observe the effect of his words.

Somewhere in the turmoil of her mind the facts connected. Of course that rumor had gotten back to him. How could she have expected that it would not? Someone had wasted no time at all to retell it and, it appeared, greatly embellish it. She realized it sounded like very damning evidence. But her anger was even greater than her humiliation at that moment.

"You have just made the most vile, despicable accusations without even bothering to ask me if they were true," she cried in a voice choked with emotion, and jumping to her feet she started backing away. "You might have had the decency and fairness to ask me first, before condemning me so readily."

Blindly, she turned and started for the door. With a couple of long strides he was beside her, a restraining grip on her arm. He forced her to face him.

"Where are you rushing to, Miss Spencer? I thought you had come here to discuss your job." His voice was menacing and the hard grip on her arm made her flinch.

"Not anymore. I don't want the job and I don't want to work for you. I just want to get away from this place. Let me go, please." Her voice shook and she despised herself for allowing him to see this weakness.

"Not until you sit back down in that chair and we finish this discussion, which, if I may remind you, you initiated."

"There is nothing I want to discuss now. Not under the circumstances," she shot at him.

"Do I take that as an admission of guilt?" he asked, the harshness in his voice increasing.

Sally looked at him and the bitterness she saw made her realize for the first time how things might have looked from his point of view. After all, many people at one time or another must have attempted

to exploit him. With such a powerful man, with so
many favors to grant, that was practically inevitable.
Perhaps he was extra sensitive to this and jumped
to the conclusion that he was being used when the
slightest evidence was presented to him.

But she was far too angry and embarrassed to consider the point for long. She wrenched her arm free.
Her green eyes held the fire of resentment as she said
between clenched teeth, "Take it as you will. But
I can assure you of at least one thing, Mr. Hawker.
I would never, under any circumstances, willingly
connect my name with yours. I too am particular about
my private life, you see."

"No, as a matter of fact that's something I don't
see. Not as long as Mike Costello is included in it."

Now they were back to that, Sally thought bitterly.
If he would only stay on one line of attack, she might
be better able to defend herself.

"Whether he is or not surely has no bearing on this
discussion," she said coldly, and could not resist adding, "unless, of course, you imagine yourself as some
sort of overlord whose underlings have to bow for
approval even in the matter of the company we keep?"

"Do you mean 'droit du seigneur,' with first rights
to every young maiden in the company?" he asked
with a wicked smile, and had the satisfaction of seeing
her blush instantly.

"Let's just keep on the subject under discussion,"
she suggested stiffly. "About this . . . rumor." She
found herself coloring violently and went on hesitantly. "I've never mentioned your name to anyone, so I
don't have the least idea how it could have started.
When I first heard it, I immediately tried to correct
it. I . . . I guess these rumors die hard," she floun-
dered, totally disconcerted by the intense interest with
which he was listening to her. "It was just as much of
a shock to me—just as abhorrent as to you . . ." The
words died out on her lips. What was the use of trying

to seem dignified if this humiliating habit of blushing gave her away every time?

Lowering her eyes, she allowed him to lead her back to her chair.

"Abhorrent is perhaps a little strong, at least as far as I'm concerned," he drawled, going around to his own chair. "Annoying was more the word I would have chosen. However, you have managed to convey to me the message that you have a great aversion to my name and in no way, be it rumor or fact, wish to be connected with it. On that basis," he added dryly, "I am prepared to believe that the whole thing started as a misunderstanding and blew out of proportion, thanks to someone's fertile imagination, as gossip has a way of doing in this place. Please accept my apology for having believed that you were responsible for something that now clearly appears to be so distasteful to you. And that brings us to the other matter at hand." All trace of amusement faded from his face now as it settled into its usual austere lines.

Sally waited, knowing that further argument was futile. If he still wanted to dismiss her, she had no choice but to accept his decision. But if she was going down, at least it had been fighting.

"I do not tolerate any reporter withholding information on a story, and I will not tolerate it from you." She saw that where the subject of his paper was concerned Rafe Hawker was a totally immovable man.

"At the same time I realize that you did not do it out of neglect, laziness, or for your own gain. You acted under the mistaken assumption that you had the right to decide what was morally fit for this paper to print. I think a little exercise in humility would serve you well as a journalist, Miss Spencer. *If* you are prepared to take it, that is," he challenged.

Sally checked the words of indignation that threatened to spring to her lips. In the first place it was ridiculously ironic that Rafe Hawker was prescribing for her, of all things, an exercise in humility. Secondly, she was being made to feel like a naughty child who had just been ordered to the principal's office to await her punishment.

Anger made her eyes sparkle but she lifted her chin and looked at him with bold defiance. She would meet any challenge he had to offer. It had become a matter of pride to do so.

"I see from that stubborn look on your face that you are prepared to take it," he observed with amusement. He measured her up speculatively, then said, "You can have your job back, though not in the city room for the time being."

He allowed a deliberate pause, then dropped the bombshell. "Our social reporter, Althea Beecham, mentioned to me recently that she was getting a little snowed under with work. I think she would be grateful for your assistance." He looked expectantly for her reaction.

This was worse than she expected, and as far as she was concerned much worse than getting fired. To be the haughty social reporter's assistant was the most distasteful job she could imagine. Meeting his glance, she was aware that he realized this full well. "An exercise in humility," he had called it, and now he was looking at her mockingly to see if she was equal to it.

She would not give him the satisfaction of letting him see how much she loathed the sentence he had just imposed on her. If it was the last thing she ever did, she would pretend that she was quite unaffected by it.

"Very well, Mr. Hawker," she said, getting up from her chair with a calmness that cost her great effort. At that moment what she felt for him bordered on hate. Her whole will was now bent toward one purpose, to rob this arrogant tyrant of the satisfaction of seeing her humiliated. "I shall start on Monday."

Erectly, she walked toward the door, but he caught up with her just as she reached it. His hand on the knob, he faced her.

"Good," he said softly, then added with his eyes lingering on her mouth, "that stiff upper lip is most becoming to you."

Helplessly, she felt herself caught up in that intense gaze, the suffocating tension she had experienced in his company once before mounting again. His eyes, so full of power, held hers and would not let go. She made a conscious effort to break away and reached for the door. Her hands met his on the doorknob and she drew back automatically as if from an electric shock.

Hawker gave a soft mocking laugh before he opened the door for her.

"I'll be keeping an eye on your progress," he murmured.

Once outside she drew a deep breath, brushing the hair back from her brow.

"Well done," the voice of Eve Tarrant broke in on her. Sally looked at her questioningly and the woman smiled.

"You have neither come out in tears, nor as pale as a ghost, which is usually the case," the secretary said with approval. "You look very much like you've held your own."

"Oh, yes, it was a real victory," Sally sighed, and it occurred to her that it was a little odd that the secretary should be congratulating her on just having done battle with her boss. Maybe it was an all-too-rare occurrence which she welcomed for reasons of her own.

"Never mind," she comforted, noting Sally's rueful look. "Did you get your job back?"

"In a manner of speaking," Sally said with a grimace. "I suppose that in itself it is some sort of an achievement." Suddenly she felt the exhaustion of the last half hour in every inch of her body.

The fact that Sally Spencer had been fired that morning had already spread through the editorial floor. That she had taken matters into her own hands by going to see the Hawk in person caused even greater astonishment among the staff. She felt curious eyes following her as she returned to her desk in the city room.

Sally was in no mood for answering the questions her colleagues were dying to ask her and she turned her back resolutely to the room. In a while, Bill McIntire walked over to her, which attracted further attention as he rarely ventured out of his busy office. He looked down at her with concern.

As Sally smiled at him, his look changed to one of relief.

"I haven't actually been thrown out onto the streets, but I have been banished from the city room," she told him, trying to keep her voice cheerful and uncaring. "I have been promoted to the exalted position of assistant to Althea Beecham."

The city editor's look was instantly sympathetic. He had no time for people like Althea, or for that matter, for the society section of the paper, and he considered exile there a heavy punishment for any reporter.

"Never mind, kid," he said, making a clumsy effort at comforting her. "You'll be back here before you know it." Then he added as an afterthought, "I'm glad you went up there after all, Sally." Self-consciously, he gave her shoulder a pat and walked away. This gave encouragement to the on-looking reporters and they started drifting over to her desk.

From their unconcealed admiration for what she had done, one would have thought she had just climbed Mount Everest, instead of the perilous heights to the twenty-fifth floor, she thought crossly. She found she had universal sympathy for her move to the social department, and the general dislike for Althea did nothing to put her mind at ease.

Sally forced herself to be busy for the remainder of her last day in the city room, doing everything possible to keep her mind from wandering to what had happened upstairs. There were so many disturbing aspects to the interview with Hawker that she knew she could not keep the thoughts at bay for long. She thought gratefully of the weekend coming up, welcoming the thought of two days grace before having to face Althea and the new job. And in those two days she would have to do some thinking.

Something in connection with Althea nagged at the back of her mind. Yes, she remembered, Hawker had said that Althea had complained to him about being snowed under with work. So the two of them *did* know each other, obviously quite well.

That would make everything fine and dandy for her, she thought with exasperation. Every move she made would probably be reported. Is that what he had meant by "keeping an eye on her progress"?

Instinctively she knew she and Althea would not get on. She remembered the woman's haughty scrutiny of her that day they met outside the elevators, and the memory sharply stirred a growing suspicion. Exactly how had Hawker heard about that unfortunate rumor? It could have been Althea who told him. It *must* have been Althea. Who else had such access to him? Who else on the paper would dare go to him and repeat gossip like that?

The more she thought about it, the more she was certain. So this was who she was to work with from now on. Her dislike turned to pure anger. Hawker obviously meant to make things so unpleasant for her —with the assistance of his socialite girl friend—that she would be forced to resign from the paper. She was now more determined than ever to ride out his challenge.

CHAPTER FIVE

Myrna Martin, Althea Beecham's secretary, greeted Sally in a state of agitation the following Monday morning.

"Dear me, this has all come so unexpectedly, I don't know what Miss Beecham will say," she told Sally disapprovingly. She was a thin, fussy, middle-aged woman who stood in nervous awe of her boss. Her one aim in life was to serve Althea as efficiently as possible.

"Don't worry about it," Sally told her cheerfully, trying to ignore the woman's ungraciousness. "Since it is all Hawker's idea, I don't expect she will say much about it."

"I don't know about that." The woman shook her head doubtfully, implying that, to her at least, the publisher's authority was not greater than Althea's. "I don't really need anyone here to help me. I've had no instructions on the matter from Miss Beecham," she continued resentfully, adding with a note of triumph, "We haven't even got a desk for you."

"Miss Beecham seems to think she needs some help, and that's why I have been transferred here," Sally replied briskly, beginning to get exasperated with the woman's resentful manner. "That small table over in the corner will do fine if no one is using it."

She waited for Miss Martin's answer but the woman only gave a sullen shrug. With an inward sigh, Sally walked to the table and began to arrange her things. The prospect of working for Althea was dismal enough, and now there was the added frustration of having to spend entire days in Miss Martin's company. As friendly as Sally was, she still decided against any further attempts to win over the stuffy secretary. She would ignore her and keep to herself as much as possible, she vowed.

It didn't take long for her to arrange the few things she had brought with her, and soon she had time to look about her with curiosity. The social department consisted of two rooms, the outer one which she was to share with the secretary, and the inner one which was Althea's. Both had touches of luxury the other editorial offices lacked. Instead of blinds, the windows were shaded by thick drapes; the overhead lights were not the usual office fixtures but had flattering, modern-looking shades, and the floors were plushly carpeted.

Miss Martin was not disposed toward conversation until she had had particular instructions from her boss as to what attitude to take toward the newcomer, so Sally sat for the next couple of hours immersed in scrapbooks of Althea Beecham's columns. When she had looked through them, she was even more disgusted with the job ahead of her than she had been before. It seemed to her that the social columns were a useless waste of space.

A sudden stirring from Miss Martin's desk warned her that someone was approaching. Despite the awkwardness of the situation, her sense of humor was triggered by the secretary's suddenly altered behavior.

Althea made a dramatic entrance into the room, a cloud of expensive and overpowering perfume drifting behind her. Sally had to admit she was an arrestingly beautiful woman, her ash-blonde hair framing a perfect face with faultless complexion and bright blue eyes. The blue silk dress she wore clung to her slim frame, flowing as she moved.

Beside her hothouse-camellia looks, Sally, with her

honey-gold hair, vivid green eyes, and peachlike complexion, looked like a healthy, sturdy sunflower.

After graciously acknowledging her secretary's fawning greetings, Althea turned blue, diamond-hard eyes in Sally's direction. "Why, who is this?" she inquired with expertly feigned surprise.

Sally let the eager Miss Martin answer the question while she coolly met Althea's insolently appraising look.

"Ah, yes," Althea said with a dismissing gesture. "I do remember Rafe mentioning something about it on the weekend. I can't imagine what he's thinking of," she added with a depreciating laugh in Sally's direction.

"I expect he was thinking of the overload of work you had complained of." Sally spoke up for the first time with perfect composure in the face of the other woman's rudeness. "At least that is how he explained it to me on Friday."

Althea's eyes narrowed as she asked in surprise. "He explained . . . to you?"

"Yes."

Althea recovered her composure and said over her shoulder as she walked into her own office, "Really, I hadn't realized Rafe was personally negotiating with his staff these days."

Sally had been prepared for haughtiness and condescension from Althea but not quite this undisguised rudeness. Miss Martin had taken it all in gleefully and now looked at her smugly from her desk in the corner.

All morning the telephones rang with call after call inviting Althea to lunches, dinners, and other social events. This was the world Althea had been born into, and although her family's circumstances had been reduced, she was now able to keep up with it through her job. Sally was beginning to wonder where she could possibly fit in in all this, when Althea called her into her office.

"I suppose I may as well give you something useful

to do," she announced graciously and added with a smile, "I don't suppose you know much about social writing."

"No, indeed," Sally agreed candidly. "I've been a newspaper reporter up to now."

The implication was not lost on Althea and a look of displeasure crossed her face. Sally knew she was not making things any easier for herself by being defiant but she would not try to ingratiate herself with this woman for any price.

Icily, Althea addressed her. "For whatever reasons of his own, Rafe has decided to transfer you here. You are not exactly the type of assistant I had in mind." Sally could well believe that. "In any case, you will find that things will be rather different for you from now on and it would be best for everyone if you tried to adjust."

It sounded like a threat but Sally was unconcerned. What did impress her was that the publisher had obviously not told Althea about the nature of Sally's disgrace and for this she felt a grudging gratitude to him.

"I shall need you to accompany me to some of the functions I attend and be handy for whatever I happen to need. It's an awful nuisance for me to have to interrupt a party to dictate my column over the telephone to my secretary, so you'll come in useful at times like that. You can take down names I give you and bring photographs back to the office. Of course," she added insinuatingly, looking at Sally's simple beige dress, "this will require some night work, so you had better get yourself some suitable dresses. Evening clothes, I mean."

"I think I have a couple of things that might do," Sally said modestly, not allowing herself to get annoyed. She was thinking in particular of two smashing evening dresses she had treated herself to on a recent shopping spree.

At that moment there was a loud knock and Althea's door was flung open. It was Mike Costello.

"I've just heard the bad news, darling," he shouted heartily, completely ignoring Althea's presence. "You'd think they could have been a little more lenient and exiled you to Siberia instead of this place." This last was unmistakably said for Althea's benefit. A look of open hostility passed between the two.

Sally had heard that Mike had briefly courted Althea, and her rejection of him had been an unforgettable blow to his ego. Althea had remained impervious to his charm because neither his social nor financial status came anywhere near her own goals. The two were reputed to be deadly enemies, as it was now evident from the atmosphere in the room. Sally had no desire to be caught in the middle.

"Miss Spencer," Althea's voice sounded brittle, "you had better take your gentleman friend out of my office and persuade him to conduct his amorous activities someplace else!"

Before Mike could retort, Sally hustled him out of the room. Outside, she exclaimed with exasperation, "You're only going to make things worse for me if you come here again. Please don't. Things are bad enough as it is."

Still furious, Mike muttered a few unflattering words in the direction of Althea's door, then said in a deliberately loud voice, "Don't let that arctic dragon depress you, Sally. She's more unpleasant than frostbite, but if the temperature gets too low for you here, just come to my office. I'll warm you up," he concluded, in a suggestive half-whisper.

They heard Miss Martin's disapproving tut-tut behind them and Mike turned around swiftly. "Myrna, my darling, I didn't notice you," he said, boisterously leaping over to the secretary's desk. Grabbing one of her struggling hands in his, he knelt by her side and gushed in mock adoration, "Did you happen to notice, Sally, that the dear lady's initials are M.M., the same as Marilyn Monroe's? I've always maintained it's not just a coincidence. It was pure foresight on her parents' part. They knew how she would turn out."

Miss Martin tugged at her hand furiously and managed an ungainly blush. Sally tried not to laugh as she told Mike in a stern voice, "That's enough horseplay now. We've got work to do, so you had better get back to your office."

Sally decided she would have to have a serious talk with him about coming to the social department again. In fact, she would have to dissuade him from being seen with her anywhere in the building, as she had no desire to be called on the carpet again for fraternizing with him during working hours. And his coming to the social department, when Althea so obviously disliked him, was an unnecessary provocation.

On Thursday morning the telephone rang and she knew from the secretary's gushing voice that it was Althea. It appeared that she wanted to speak with Sally, so she took the phone.

"I will be needing you at the play opening tonight," she announced regally. "I shall have some names and things to send back with you during intermission. However, you need not dress up. You can wait for me in the lobby and I shall meet you there after the first act."

Sally decided against going home and filled in time looking around the shops until it was time to walk over to the theater on Broadway. It was a stiflingly hot evening and when she emerged from one of her favorite shops, a summer storm had begun. Sally had no umbrella or coat with her and by the time she got to the theater she was soaked to the skin, her thin summer dress clinging to her body. She made a dash for the ladies' room to try to repair some of the damage the rain had caused.

There was little she could do about her wet dress but she made an attempt to wipe her sandals clean and tidy her hair, which clung to her head in curly tendrils. She ran a comb through it but the curls sprang stubbornly back, so, giving up, she patted her face with a towel and applied fresh lipstick.

Back in the lobby she passed the time until intermission by looking at the photographs and old playbills on the walls, and soon the crowd came streaming out.

Sally felt conspicuously out of place among the long gowns, furs, and dinner suits of the premiere-night crowd. She searched the faces for Althea's, hoping to get away from there as soon as possible, and finally she saw the woman coming toward her.

Even in that glittering crowd she stood out. Her blonde hair was piled on top of her head, secured with a dazzling diamond clip, which Sally supposed was a remnant of the family fortune. Her pearly skin was beautifully contrasted by the sapphire-blue chiffon gown falling in soft folds about her. Althea looked at Sally's somewhat bedraggled appearance with displeasure.

"Really, when I said you need not dress, I did not mean you should show up like this—" With a distasteful wave of her hand, she let the sentence trail significantly.

"I was caught in the rain," replied Sally impatiently. She had no wish to engage in a discussion on appearances in the middle of the crowded lobby. "The sooner you give me whatever you have to send back to the office, the sooner I can leave and stop embarrassing you," she told her tersely.

The look of disapproval lingered on Althea's perfectly made-up face as she handed Sally a list of names that were to be added to her column, which the printers were waiting at that moment to set. "You had better leave now," she urged Sally, who was only too happy to oblige.

"Not before she has a drink to ward off a chill," a deep voice drawled behind them.

Sally tensed, for a moment unwilling to turn around.

"Rafe, I thought you were at the bar," Althea

purred, her face instantly taking on a radiant glow.

Sally felt a terror shoot through her but she forced herself to turn around and say calmly, "Hello, Mr. Hawker."

He nodded in greeting, his eyes taking in her rain-molded dress and sleek wet hair, but not with the same disapproval Althea had shown.

"Very few girls look as well ravaged by rain as Miss Spencer, don't you think?" he addressed the blonde woman by his side, amusement gleaming in his eyes. Althea tried to laugh as if this were some private joke between the two of them but she did not quite succeed. Her annoyance at Hawker's apprecia-tive glance at Sally was obvious.

There was a tense moment of silence between the two women, though Hawker himself looked perfectly at ease. Sally noticed how well he looked in his severe black dinner suit. He was the only man in the lobby who did not look dressed up; he looked as natural and comfortable in evening dress as other men did in jeans. The black evening jacket highlighted the gray threads beginning to show in his hair, and the crisp whiteness of his shirt front, buttoned with plain gold studs, accentuated his tan. Sally had never before considered him truly handsome but now her heart took a leap at the sight of him, towering head and shoulders over the crowd around him.

"I had better get you a drink, Miss Spencer, or you will catch cold." His voice was smooth and Sally was not quite sure if she detected a slight mocking under-tone to it. Her protest of "No, thank you, I'd better be going," died out unheeded as he took the two women lightly by the elbow and propelled them to-ward the bar. She noticed how easy it was for him to get through a crowd. People seemed to respectfully part before his approach.

He left them in a remote corner and made his way with equal ease to the bar.

"This is turning into quite an evening for you,

isn't it?" Althea turned on her suddenly and Sally was taken aback by the hint of venom in her voice.

"Not really," she replied nonchalantly, deliberately misunderstanding. "I've often been to the theater before."

The blonde woman made an audible sound of anger but Hawker was already on his way back to them. He was followed by a waiter carrying safely above his head a small silver tray with their drinks. No one else in the crowd had elicited such service.

Althea was immediately impressed and said admiringly, "Darling, how on earth did you manage it?" She sipped at her champagne daintily and looked at him invitingly over the rim of her glass.

"With a very large tip," Hawker replied dryly. Sally smiled in spite of herself and almost liked him at that moment. He might be flagrant about using his power but at least he was not pretentious about it.

Althea began chatting about the play and drawing Rafe's attention to their mutual friends in the crowded room. Hawker was politely, if a little remotely, attentive and the conversation effectively excluded Sally.

She noted with interest the alteration in Althea's behavior whenever the publisher was near. Usually so forbidding and haughty, she was positively simpering and coy in the man's company. This, Sally thought wryly, was bound to be an error in tactics. She was sure Hawker would be much more impressed by supercilious haughtiness than female archness. Still, who was she to judge? It seemed to be working for Althea; after all, she *was* his constant companion, wasn't she?

She found the thought surprisingly disturbing and wondered how soon she could get away. Sipping her drink, she prayed silently for the bell to announce the end of intermission.

As if reading her mind, Rafe Hawker turned to her. "I expect you are anxious to get back to the paper to finish your work."

A little disconcerted by this abrupt dismissal, Sally nodded in agreement. Althea, on the other hand, glowed with pleasure and put a possessive hand on her companion's arm.

"Yes, run along, Sally. I shall see you at the office tomorrow," she waved in dismissal.

Choking back anger and humiliation, Sally said good night stiffly and turned on her heels to go, but Hawker moved quickly into her path.

"I'd better see you through this crowd," he said with determination, already propelling her toward the door.

Sally's glance instinctively flew to the other woman's face. Althea's smile had frozen and her eyes were lit with hatred. Her icy "Don't miss the curtain, Rafe darling," appeared to have been unheard by him.

As Hawker guided her through the crowd his light touch on her arm felt like a burning vise, and she felt overwhelmed by his nearness.

"It's raining heavily," he observed at the entrance, keeping his hold on her. She felt as if every nerve in her body were concentrated in that one spot. "I have a car waiting somewhere about. I'll have the chauffeur drop you off."

Resenting the sureness of his voice and the way his closeness made her feel, she told him primly, "I don't think that is a very good idea. It might add fuel to those rumors."

The moment the words were out she regretted them. She realized it sounded like a cheap shot, quite un-called for in view of his politeness in offering to send her home in his own car. For a brief second he looked at her in surprise, then his hand on her arm tightened and a shadow passed across his eyes.

Then he was his usual mocking self as he said, "I can take them if you can." He paused long enough to enjoy the confusion this created in her and added, "Besides, if you caught cold, who would take care of you with your Aunt Emily so far away?" Again

Sally was surprised by the keenness of his memory.

Surprise soon changed to anger when he added as a sarcastic afterthought, "Though, of course, your friend Mike Costello has a considerable reputation for his bedside manner."

Sally was too angry and bewildered by the constant contradictions in his personality to reply. He could change so abruptly from politeness to arrogance, from concern to sarcasm. One moment he was being gallant by putting his chauffeur at her disposal, the next he was attacking her with sarcastic suggestions.

She felt more than usually angry at this latest attack. For a moment tonight she had actually felt something for him. She had almost liked the man. That would teach her to be taken in so easily by his infrequent pleasantries.

She would have gladly broken away from him then and hailed a cab but he had already motioned to his driver, and the shiny limousine was just drawing up at the entrance. He held the door open for her and, when she was seated inside, leaned in the front window beside the driver.

"Bob, this is Miss Spencer. Drive her to the Globe Building and wait until she has finished her work. Then drive her straight home. You can pick us up at the restaurant after the theater," he instructed.

Before Sally had time to speak, he had already waved an impersonal farewell and disappeared inside the theater.

Their progress was slow through the chaotic traffic of nighttime Broadway, and Sally had plenty of time to think. As always after any meeting with Hawker, she found herself agitated, her thoughts in a turmoil. He managed to arouse so many emotions in one brief encounter and always left her with plenty of contradictions to work out. Sinking back against the expensive leather upholstery, she tried to make sense of this latest gesture of his.

Wasn't it only a few days ago that he had accused

her of making use of his name to advance her career on the paper? Now he was having her chauffeured around in his private limousine, instructing his driver to wait until she had completed her work and to drive her home afterward. Detection of her in his car by any one of the staff would be enough to set the whole paper ablaze with gossip.

And the episode in the theater was equally confusing. He had insisted that she join them for a drink when he must have sensed the tension and dislike between the two women. Maybe that was it, she speculated suspiciously. Maybe he liked to create friction and was amused by the discomfort it caused. Had he even used her to irritate Althea for some perverse reason of his own?

When the car reached the Globe building, she turned to the driver. "There really is no need for you to wait around for me. I can easily catch a cab when I've finished work."

"I'd better wait for you, miss, if the boss says so," the driver returned doggedly, leaving no room for argument. Sally felt a twinge of irritation. Why did everyone have to take Hawker's word as unshakable law? Still, there was no point in taking it out on the driver; he was only doing his job and she did not wish him to get into trouble on her account.

"I'll be as quick as I can then," she told him, loath to keep anyone waiting.

"Take all the time you need, miss," the driver replied placidly.

Sally finished her work in less than an hour and the limousine, as instructed, was still waiting for her outside. She ducked into it quickly, rather embarrassed at the thought that one of her late-working colleagues might see her.

When she had settled inside and they were back in the stream of traffic, she ventured to ask the driver, "Have you worked for Mr. Hawker for long?"

"Five years, miss," he replied. She stifled the urge

to question him further, much as she would have liked to have some light shed on the mysterious Mr. Hawker.

"What about you, miss, have you worked on *The Globe* for long?"

"Only a few weeks. I worked on a much smaller paper before that."

"How do you like it?"

"Very much, most of the time," she said dryly.

"I'm sure you'll do very well, miss," the driver said after a thoughtful silence.

"I certainly hope you're right, but how can you be so sure?" she laughed.

"You've got that look about you," he replied, and smiled with approval at her reflection in the rearview mirror. "Like you really enjoy your job. You don't look as sullen and dissatisfied with things as so many young people do these days. Besides, the boss must think a lot of you. He doesn't usually get me to drive his reporters around. Except for that other lady, the blonde one that writes about all that society stuff."

Later that night, after Bob had dropped her off, she sat sipping a cup of coffee in her darkened room. Her mind raked over the irony of the situation. She and Hawker had nothing but antagonism for each other. They could barely keep on civil terms for the length of a conversation. Yet here she was, working in uncomfortably close proximity with Althea, who seemed to look on her as some sort of threat and was getting more malicious toward her every day.

For the thousandth time since she first met him, Sally wished she could lock Hawker out of her mind. But as usual, she drifted, in spite of herself, toward those rare moments when antagonisms were forgotten and he had a different look in his eyes, a look that made her want to get to know the real Rafe Hawker.

There was that first time in his car outside her home in Glenbrook when for a suspended second she felt herself drowning in the intensity of his gaze; then the time in his office a few days ago when the slightest contact of their hands was a scorching shock to her body; and again tonight, when she had managed to provoke him to anger for a brief instant and his grip on her arm had tightened. She felt shame for her weakness in dwelling on those moments and told herself that they were of no significance at all to him, and in all likelihood were forgotten the second they were over.

Full of scorn for her foolishness, she forced herself to look at the facts. And the facts were that he and Althea were in a nightclub even now, enjoying an after-theater supper, or were perhaps in each other's arms somewhere on a crowded dance floor.

Dragging her mind away from this unwelcome picture, she undressed quickly and stepped under the shower. She stayed a long time under the soothing caress of the water, waiting for it to wash away the tension of the whole day.

It was a long time before she was able to fall asleep, however. How was it possible, she puzzled, that the memory of a man for whom she felt nothing but dislike could rob her of so many nights of sleep?

As she had expected, the atmosphere in the social department the next day was a little chilly. Mid-morning Althea swept in and made a deliberate show of ignoring Sally. Instead she turned to Miss Martin to tell her with a daintily concealed yawn, "I'm staying only a few minutes. I'm quite dead on my feet since I practically danced them off last night and only got to bed a few hours ago. Do be an angel and hold off my calls. Except, of course," she called gaily over her shoulder, "if Mr. Hawker calls. Ah, all that champagne . . ." Her voice trailed as she disappeared into her office.

Not long after, Althea emerged from her office and, having given a few orders to the secretary, she prepared to leave. At the door she stopped and, pretending to recall something, she came and stood by Sally's table.

"I might not have made myself quite clear about your duties," she said with an attempt at indifference; but her eyes were sharply unpleasant. "Socializing is my job, not yours. When you come along to these functions, you are merely there as my assistant, not one of the guests. Last night at the theater, for example," she paused, gesturing with her jeweled hands, "it was really completely unnecessary for you to join us for drinks."

Sally, who had been expecting just such an attack, responded with a self-assurance she did not feel. "I thought so too. But as you witnessed yourself, Mr. Hawker was insistent, and I for one am not prepared to force an argument with my employer in a crowded theater lobby."

"Perhaps, my dear," Althea threw at her between tightly drawn lips, "you should learn the difference between an invitation extended from mere courtesy and one that is genuinely meant." Without waiting for a reply, she stalked out of the room.

CHAPTER SIX

Sally had been making a deliberate attempt to avoid Mike Costello, both in the office and after working hours. Contact with him at *The Globe* had brought nothing but trouble, trouble she was determined not to provoke again. When he rang her at home and

tried to make a date, she put him off with vague
excuses. She knew he was dying of curiosity and
wanted a firsthand account of the events leading up
to her working in the social department, but she had
not been in the mood to give him explanations.

One morning she heard hurried footsteps behind
her in the office corridor. Mike caught up with her
and took a possessive hold of her arm.

"Slow down there, beautiful, I want to talk to you,"
he said, determination gleaming in his blue eyes.

"Not right now, please, Mike. I have things to do."
She tried to shrug his hand off impatiently, not want-
ing to be engaged in a conversation with him right
there in the corridor.

"That's what you've been saying for weeks now
and I'd like to know the reason why," he insisted. "If
you don't want to talk to me here, then come out with
me tonight. This time I won't take no for an answer."

Sally was annoyed but didn't wish a confrontation
with him. She could clearly see Mike meant it when
he said he would not take no for an answer.

"All right," she agreed reluctantly. "Tonight, then."

Mike's grin was victorious and he gave her hand a
meaningful squeeze. "I'll pick you up at seven, Sally.
Put on your best rags. I'm taking you somewhere
fancy."

Sally winced. She hated his glib manner and thought
that for all his imagined suaveness and sophistication,
he came across to her as predictably and transparently
as any of the small-town boys she knew.

Getting ready for her date that night Sally chided
herself for her ungraciousness to Mike in the past
few weeks. She had barely been civil to him, she
recalled with regret. It was true that he often irritated
her and sometimes made her downright angry with
his impertinence, but lately she seemed to be taking
all her annoyances out on him. She wondered why he
still wanted to take her out when there were so many
other girls much more eager for his company.

As she slipped into one of her new evening gowns

she began to relax. The evening could be enjoyable after all and it had been ages since she had gone out. Running Althea's social errands on so many nights of the week was enough to make her want to spend her free evenings at home alone.

She looked with satisfaction at her reflection in the mirror. The dress had been an extravagance which now she did not regret. It was made of alternate layers of gray and palest pink organdy, joined by silver metallic thread. From two thin straps it cascaded in frothy clouds down her slender body. The dress was utterly feminine, and suited her perfectly. With it she wore silver sandals, and a silver evening purse lay ready on her bed. She swept her hair up in a soft curly cloud, leaving her slender neck exposed and ornamented by a thin platinum chain with a pearl and diamond drop that had belonged to her mother. There was enough female vanity in Sally to be buoyed by the fact that she was looking her best tonight. She only wished her date was someone in whom she was more interested.

When Mike arrived for her, his eyes roved over her in frank admiration. "You are the most beautiful creature I ever saw," he whistled. "I'll be able to show you off to perfection in the Chantilly Room."

The restaurant was one of the most expensive in New York, on top of a skyscraper with breathtaking views of the whole of Manhattan. Mike was so busy admiring Sally that it was not until they were seated at the bar sipping their cocktails that he brought up what was in the back of his mind.

"Isn't it time you brought me up to date on what the hell is going on?" he began bluntly. "One minute you're in the city room with a front-page story to your name, and the next I hear you've been fired. To contradict all that, I find you a few days later in the social department, of all places."

Sally realized it was time she leveled with Mike, for her own sake as much as his. Maybe it would set him straight about one or two things once and for all. She told him briefly all that had led up to her banishment to Althea's domain. Mike listened with shrewd attentiveness, his mind busily calculating how much he should read between the lines.

"As you can see," Sally concluded, "that puts an end to all your suspicions and insinuations about Mr. Hawker and me. Even *your* devious mind can't read any romantic significance into the fact that he fired me."

Mike, for the moment at least, appeared satisfied with the explanation, and Sally hoped she would be able to enjoy the rest of the evening without further cross-examination.

At Mike's insistence, they ordered the most lavish items on the menu. He took great delight in spending money ostentatiously, and although Sally would frankly have preferred some of the simpler dishes, she let him order for her. Boosted by the excellent food and wine, Mike's spirits were at their highest and he was making a conscious effort to be very entertaining company.

After the lengthy meal he took Sally to the dance floor. He was an easy and stylish dancer and Sally, with her natural grace, matched him perfectly. Admiring glances followed them about the floor, which inspired Mike to show off even more than usual.

Sally was quite out of breath when he finally led her back to their table. To her astonishment, Mike had hardly seated himself when he brought up their earlier topic of conversation.

"You might think there is nothing extraordinary in the fact that you were able to charm the immovable Mr. Hawker into giving your job back," he began without preliminaries, "but I believe it is a feat never before accomplished by anyone else."

Sally glared at him incredulously. Had the subject of Hawker been churning through his mind all that time they were dancing? Did the man never let up on anything?

"Maybe no one else has ever tried," she suggested, adding with sarcasm, "Besides, wouldn't it be an unnecessarily elaborate way of showing his interest in me to fire me just so he could hire me back?"

Mike shrugged the question off and continued, "It certainly puts you in an awkard position, having to work with Althea."

"It's not the pleasantest job I've ever had," she agreed.

"You do know that she's after Hawker and determined to get him, don't you?"

Suddenly Sally could stand the conversation no longer. "I wouldn't know anything about that since I'm hardly in the confidence of either of them," she said impatiently, and forestalled something Mike was about to say. "I was having a nice evening. Do you think we could continue it by leaving Mr. Hawker out of it?"

"That might be a little difficult under the circumstances," Mike hissed, his voice suddenly full of excitement, his eyes straining toward a far corner. Sally involuntarily followed his glance just in time for her eyes to meet Rafe Hawker's across the room.

He had just been shown to his table in the company of a large party and was still standing, holding a chair back for the woman at his side. He gave Sally a slight bow.

She jerked her head away as if she had just been struck a heavy blow. Damn, she thought, if only he hadn't caught her looking at him. Mike was too fascinated with the publisher's sudden appearance to notice her violent blush. The coincidence of the meeting hit her at once and she looked at Mike with quick suspicion.

"This could prove very interesting," he smirked with relish.

"It wasn't deliberately arranged by you, by any chance?" she demanded.

All at once he was the picture of hurt innocence.

"How can you accuse me of such a thing?" he protested. "The whole thing is a fantastic coincidence.
Just when we were discussing him, too."

"We always seem to be doing that," she replied with
resentment, adding crossly, "I don't see why you look
so pleased about it all, anyway." But to herself Sally
agreed that it was a fantastic coincidence, though
probably not all that surprising. The restaurant was
one of the best in the city, and was probably one of
his regular hangouts. Well, she wasn't going to be
made to feel guilty and embarrassed just because she
happened to be dining in the same restaurant.

No matter how firmly she resolved to ignore his
presence and to carry on the evening as before, her
nerves seemed frazzled and she felt her pulse beating
heavily. In the split second that she had turned
around, she had noted that the dinner party did not
include Althea but seemed to be made up of rather
stout, middle-aged people. In any case, she didn't care
who he was dining with, she reminded herself.

Finally, Mike had the discretion to stop his ogling
in the other table's direction and returned his attentions to her. He became very animated as if trying to
prove to everyone in the room what a good time the
two of them were having. When he asked her to
dance, she declined.

A knowing smile flashed into Mike's eyes. "Do you
think he would mind seeing you in my arms?" he
teased.

She was in no mood to be teased, however, and
suggested, "We could leave and make it more comfortable all around."

"Don't you think that might be a little obvious?" he
asked, and she had to agree that it was a foolish idea.
"Besides," he added wickedly, "I'm not in the least
uncomfortable."

Sally noted with alarm that Mike was taking great
pleasure in the situation and she had the sinking feeling he did not mean to go unnoticed by Hawker tonight. She felt hopelessly trapped and toyed with the

idea of disappearing into the ladies' room, but realized if she got up from the table she would only draw attention to herself. At the same time she felt angry with herself for allowing the awesome Mr. Hawker to spoil her evening merely by being in the room.

She forced herself to relax and carry on a normal conversation with Mike, though with his interest partly elsewhere that was not easy. All of a sudden his eyes lit up and with a muttered "here we go," he fixed a welcoming smile on his face.

Every nerve in Sally's body was signaling Hawker's approach to their table. She fought down a rising panic, and by the time he reached them, she was outwardly composed, only the tightly clenched hands in her lap giving proof of how far her self-control was being taxed.

"Good evening," Rafe Hawker drawled. The greeting was for both of them but his eyes were on Sally, ignoring Mike, who had sprung to his feet. A hovering waiter, whose attention had been commanded by his imposing figure, hurried up with an extra chair. For a brief second Sally hoped he would refuse it and after his greeting pass on his way, but he accepted the chair.

"Do you mind?" he asked coolly.

"Not at all," Mike replied promptly and Sally winced at the eagerness in his voice. It was in direct contrast to Hawker's own lazy, self-assured tone.

"Having a staff conference?" he asked, his eyes boring into Sally's. It was rudely obvious he meant to exclude Mike from the conversation.

Mike did not appear to notice that Hawker was deliberately ignoring him and said, "You could say we were discussing matters connected with the paper."

"Anything in particular, Costello?" the publisher inquired, turning cold eyes at him. Mike had started out on a note of impertinence but Hawker's direct mocking gaze seemed to unnerve him and he went on a little more hesitantly.

"Oh, mostly about Sally's new job. She was telling

me what an experience it is to work with Miss Beecham." Mike's slightly nervous smile belied his cocky manner.

"And what sort of experience do you find it, Miss Spencer?" He turned back to her with a look of amusement.

"Unforgettable would be a good way of describing it," Sally returned evenly. If he expected complaints from her, he was in for a disappointment.

There was a moment of silence and Sally wondered if Hawker would take his leave now. But no, he was too self-confident to be made uneasy by such a thing as a lapse in conversation.

It was Mike who made an attempt to close the uncomfortable pause and began talking rapidly. Sally tried to keep up her end of the conversation but Hawker sat back without making the least effort to join in. He did no more than respond with a clipped monosyllable whenever Mike addressed a sentence to him. Mike became more and more nervous as, losing his earlier confidence, he began talking too fast and too loud. Sally felt a searing humiliation for him, realizing that he was making a fool of himself, and the full force of her anger was directed against Hawker, who, in her opinion, was behaving with unforgivable rudeness.

If he was going to sit there letting the other two make the best of an awkward situation he himself had created, she wished he would go back to his table at once. A tension was growing about the table and finally she could take it no longer.

"If you will excuse me for a moment," she blurted, and without waiting for their response hurried off to the ladies' room. She realized she had sounded slightly hysterical running off like that but she could not help it. If she had been alone, she would have given Hawker what he deserved by lapsing into a silence to match his own until he would have been forced to go away. But Mike obviously had no such command over himself and she could not bear to watch him make a fool of himself for another moment.

Her face looked tense and drawn in the powder-room mirror and she added blush and some fresh lipstick for a little more color. She hoped that while she was away Mike would have the sense to see that Hawker's aim was to unnerve him and would act less anxious to entertain him. Where had Mike's usual insolence and self-assurance gone? Did Hawker have this effect on everyone? If the situation had not improved by the time she got back, she would insist that Mike take her home. She was ready to feign a headache or use any other ploy she could think of to get away from there. She lingered a little longer, but regrettably she could not hide out in the powder room forever.

As she approached the table she saw with a sinking heart that Mike was not there. She did not relish being left alone with Hawker and hoped that Mike would be back soon.

Hawker rose and pulled back her chair for her. "Mr. Costello sends his regrets. He had to leave suddenly," he announced smoothly, as if he were telling her nothing more important than that the restaurant was out of the wine they had ordered.

As her eyes flew to his face, she saw a faint, derisive smile twist his lips. She was so astonished and angry that she did not even notice him forcibly push her down into her chair. He took the seat beside her.

"Don't look so alarmed," he said with an insolence that made her cheeks burn with indignation. "I assured Mr. Costello that I would see you safely home."

"Did you indeed!" She exploded with all the anger that had been building inside her and almost choked on her words. "And what sort of intimidation did you use to make him leave so suddenly?"

Hawker looked at her without concern. "It was persuasion, rather than intimidation. Why should Mike Costello be intimidated by me?" he shrugged.

"He's a man and should be able to stand up to me."
He added with harshness in his voice, "But it's not in
his character. He's too anxious to get to the top to
let his pride get in his way. Don't worry, Mike Costello is no stranger to intimidation. He uses it himself, but only on people who can't fight him back."

Even in the depths of her anger, Sally felt the truth
of his words. What he was saying was no more than
she herself had discerned about Mike. Character had
never been the most outstanding thing about him.
Look how he had deserted her, she told herself with
humiliation. He had simply walked out and left her
in the company of this man.

But to Hawker she said, "I'm not going to sit here
and listen to you belittle another man's character
when you have behaved tonight with the most arrogant display of rudeness I have ever witnessed in my
life. While you are on the subject of character, what
have you to say about your own? What sort of character does it take to deliberately make someone look
small in public?"

"So Mike Costello looked small to you, did he?" he
shot at her with unexpected vehemence. "I'm delighted to hear it. Had he been in anyone else's company I would not have bothered to, as you put it,
'belittle' him. But since it was you, I considered the
effort well worthwhile. You've been so stubborn about
him, I thought I'd let you see him in an unflattering
light."

"Well thank you so much for the distinction," she
returned, her green eyes burning, "but that is too
presumptuous even for you. It is hardly your place to
do that. I'm sure you would be outraged if anyone
dared to point out the shortcomings of someone with
whom *you* were keeping company."

"Go right ahead," he invited, a hint of amusement
playing at the corners of his mouth. "Who, for instance?"

Sally bit her lip and flushed slightly. She had almost

stepped into a trap then, and she had the uncomfortable feeling he had understood that her veiled reference had been to Althea. Hawker gave one of his soft, nerve-racking laughs and she was certain he had read her mind.

"Would you like to dance?" The question came so unexpectedly that she was taken completely by surprise. At once she knew that she wanted to very much, and she felt a bit ashamed. She wanted to know how it felt in his arms, what it would be like to be held by him in the closeness of the crowded dance floor.

"No, I certainly would not," she told him stubbornly instead. "I would like to go home now, unless, of course, you intend to try some of your bullying on me, too."

"Don't tempt me," he laughed softly, and her heart gave a wild leap at the look he gave her.

He was already on his feet and waiting for her to rise when she remembered something. "Your companions must be wondering what has happened to you."

"I said good night to them before I came to join you," he replied evenly.

"Were you that certain of the outcome of this evening?" She could not hold the resentful question back.

"Yes," he replied matter-of-factly, and her heart lurched again. "I'll take you home. It's the least I can do for the poor intimidated Mr. Costello," he added with a slow, impertinent smile.

Sally was furious, but to argue the point with him now would make her seem childishly sullen. Besides, she still carried a deep resentment against Mike for having abandoned her so readily. With her mouth set and her brows drawn together in a frown, she allowed him to escort her from the room.

In the mirrored hallway she caught a glimpse of herself, her eyes unnaturally bright, her cheeks flushed. Anger, she told herself while her hand auto-

matically flew up to tuck away a wisp of unruly
curl. Her eyes met his reflection towering above her.

"You look very lovely," he told her and she quickly
looked away.

They rode the elevator in silence to the basement
garage. Sally had not counted on this and had resolved to take her leave of him in the lobby of the
building, catching a cab home. But now that they
were here, she could not very well run off. One of
the garage attendants brought his car to the entrance
and handed him the keys. She wondered why his
chauffeur wasn't driving, when Hawker himself explained.

"Bob is off tonight. He'll be very sorry he missed
you. It seems you made a very favorable impression
on him when he drove you home the other night."

After she had given him her address, they drove
on in silence. Of all his moods, she found his silence
the most unnerving, yet she was afraid of breaking
it in case her voice betrayed her mounting tension.

Outside her apartment house he slid the car to a
halt, turned the motor off, and looked at her expectantly.

Sally said with emphasis, and not altogether free of
sarcasm, "Thank you so much for all the trouble you
have taken with me this evening. I don't want to keep
you longer than necessary."

"It was no trouble to me at all, but since you think
it was, you might care to make amends by giving
me some coffee," he said, already moving to get out
of the car. Before he opened the door he turned to
her with one of his half-concealed smiles and said
deliberately, "Don't worry. I won't be kept longer
than necessary."

Sally felt a mixture of annoyance and panic. Did
Rafe Hawker really mean to come up to her apartment? When he had helped her out of the car, she
walked stiffly to the front door.

"I live on the top floor. . . . There's no elevator. It's

a four-floor walk-up." She wasn't quite sure what she hoped to accomplish with this warning.

"That does not deter me in the least," he returned with a touch of humor, leading the way up the winding stairs in easy loping strides. Outside her door he took the key from her and pushed it into the lock. She had noticed on other occasions these touches of almost old-fashioned courtesy about him, and again she wondered at his complex personality.

Hawker looked around the low-ceilinged room as he stood there for a moment after she had turned the light on. Haltingly, she invited him to take a seat while she went to put her wrap and evening purse away, but he began pacing about the room instead, examining everything about him with curiosity.

Sally went into the kitchen to grind fresh coffee and was at the sink filling up the percolator with water when she sensed, rather than saw, him in the doorway.

"You appear to be an excellent housekeeper," he commented, looking around with approval at her spotless kitchen.

"Have you been running your fingers along my furniture for traces of dust?" she asked caustically, bending deeper over the sink to avoid his eyes. A lock of hair worked itself free and fell over her forehead. Her hands full, she tossed back her head trying to get the offending hair out of her eyes.

Hawker stepped forward and tucked the lock back for her, holding it for a moment, feeling its silken texture. She shivered at the unexpected touch and turned away abruptly. She had felt only the slightest touch of his hand but it was enough to create a wild flutter in her heart. By the time she went back to turn off the tap, he had left the kitchen.

While the coffee was percolating Sally went into the living room to set up a tray with cups, saucers, cream, and sugar. Hawker lounged in a chair with his long legs thrust out before him. His eyes followed her about the room, succeeding in making her feel self-conscious.

When she had poured out his coffee, he took an appreciative sip and commented, "You're one of the few women who know how to make really good coffee."

Sally refused to acknowledge the compliment. She was certainly not going to trouble herself as a hostess tonight. She hadn't invited him here, hadn't wanted him to come, so she would let him make all the effort in conversation. She would pay him back for his own rude silence at the restaurant earlier that night.

Hawker did not appear to take note of her reticence and continued talking with ease. "Has this apartment adequate security?" he inquired. Sally resented the question as she resented everything about him. What would have seemed solicitude in others seemed merely condescension in him.

"Quite," she snapped and, instantly regretting her rudeness, amended, "At least, it's as safe as any apartment in this city."

"New York is safe enough if you abide by its rules," he said conversationally. "But I noticed you don't have a security guard at the front door and I think it would be wise to install an extra safety lock on your own door." Practical advice of this sort was so out of keeping with Rafe Hawker that she couldn't help a quick smile of amusement.

Hawker caught her look and smiled back at her. The gesture, once again unexpected, sent a wave of heat over her skin and she looked away. It was the first time that she had seen a genuine smile on his face, without a trace of its usual cynicism.

Whether understanding her embarrassment, or for another reason, Hawker tactfully moved to another subject. "Have you heard from Mr. Smith recently?" he asked.

"Yes, only last week," Sally replied, eagerly accepting the new subject. "I write to him fairly often but he, like most journalists, hates writing letters and telephones me instead. He is very well and tells me *The Patriot* is running as smoothly as ever."

"You two appear to have a particularly close relationship. He takes a fatherly pride in you." Sally nodded but made no comment.

"And your Aunt Emily? How is she?"

Sally stole a suspicious look at him. "For someone you have never met, she seems to arouse your interest a great deal. You've referred to her more than once now," she said, puzzled. She wouldn't put it past this man to find some sort of amusement in her small-town family.

"It's true I've never met her . . . yet I think I know exactly what she would be like," he answered after a thoughtful pause. "She is probably all that I never knew in my aunt or any other relative. When I was a kid, I spent a lot of time with my nose pressed against the windows of houses like your Aunt Emily's. Looking in from the outside."

Sally was completely disarmed by his candid reply and noted both bitterness and wistfulness in his voice. Could this be where Rafe Hawker's secret lay, somewhere in his childhood? Was there something sad in that childhood that had molded the guarded, unapproachable adult of today? She waited eagerly for him to go on, to reveal something of the unknown man behind the facade, but he noticed her searching look and gave a short laugh.

"I could really take you in with a hard-luck story if I wanted to, couldn't I? I can see you're a soft touch for them. However, I won't. Instead I would like to hear more about your family and your life in Glenbrook."

Sally felt herself slowly drawn into talking about her life in the cozy, loving shelter of the Holloway home, and the joys and frustrations of life in the spic-and-span, ordered atmosphere of the small country town.

She talked about her parents, her childhood years,

about her aunt, uncle, and five cousins. Feeling very much at ease now, she even told him about the old weeping willow, a secret she had never shared with anyone else.

Through it all, Hawker sat forward in his chair listening intently, his face for once devoid of cynicism. His searching gaze became so intense that Sally, suddenly self-conscious, stopped abruptly. She was amazed at how easily he had compelled her to talk freely, while he still remained a tightly locked mystery.

Her hand fluttered helplessly as their eyes locked, but this time his stare was not overpowering or commanding. She realized with a heart-stopping awareness that he had been caught just as much off-guard as she.

Hawker was the first to recover from the moment and, slowly, a shielding veil drew over his eyes. In her embarrassment, Sally moved too quickly and knocked a coffee cup off the table, which landed with a nerve-tingling crash. Before Hawker could stoop to retrieve it, she was on her hands and knees, gathering it up.

She dabbed nervously at the stain on the rug by his feet, glad of being able to hide her face.

In the next instant her heart seemed to stop as her breath caught in her throat. Hawker, leaning over her, touched lightly the spot where her thick hair brushed across the nape of her neck. Leaning still further, his lips descended and he kissed the spot softly.

Sally's arms sagged and she felt too weak to support her own body. This time it was not the familiar electric shock but an aching wave that washed over her. His indescribably tender gesture left her drained of all strength. For a second she remained kneeling on the floor; in the next, she felt his hands on her arms, pulling her gently up to the chair beside his.

Not one of his gestures of arrogance and aggression

could have left her feeling as vulnerable as this completely unexpected, utterly alien tenderness. If he had wanted to kiss her at all, she would have expected it to be in his usual cruel, overpowering, mocking way.

Sally was so absorbed in this newly aroused, disturbing sensation that she hardly noticed him rise and go to the kitchen. He returned with a wet cloth and finished mopping up the coffee stain.

When he finished, he looked up at her with a smile that was guarded once more, and teased, "That's better. I can't have you groveling at my feet like that, can I, Miss Spencer?" Her heart ached at the thought that he had recovered so quickly and was now making a joke of the matter. It was either great tact or self-defense which had made him switch moods already.

"I thought that was where you preferred everyone, Mr. Hawker . . . at your feet," she returned, trying to match his light tone though everything inside her was aching for the moment that had passed. Only a slight tremor of her hands and her still wide, glistening eyes betrayed what had just happened.

Hawker's face was again an expressionless mask and she wondered with a sinking heart if he was already regretting his moment of weakness. For that was no doubt how he would sooner or later regard his action, she thought bitterly. Why was he able to compose himself so much more easily than she? Sally wondered with resentment.

"No, not at my feet," he now laughed in answer. "As a matter of fact, I prefer most people at a comfortable arm's length." Was that meant for me? she wondered, feeling pain at his seeming indifference.

"I imagine most people try their best to oblige you there," she continued with effort.

"Do you . . . try?" His smile was challenging.

"Yes," she met it boldly. Inevitably they were returning to the earlier mood of the evening, as if what had just passed between them had been dreamed by her, that kiss nothing more than a feverish part of the dream, something of which he now appeared to be totally unaware. The speed with which he could change the tone of his voice and the meaning of his glance spun her head dizzyingly.

Too much on edge now to sit still, Sally got up from her chair with a restless motion which Hawker chose to interpret as his cue to leave. He was immediately on his feet.

"Thank you for your excellent coffee," he said with a politeness that emphasized the void between them. He moved to the door with Sally following, and they almost collided when he turned. "In case you are expecting an apology for earlier this evening, I won't be making one," he informed her with arrogance. "The fact is, I'm not in the least sorry that I broke up your evening out with Mike Costello."

The remark had the effect of immediately bringing Sally back to reality. That part of the evening seemed so far away now that she had almost forgotten it; it seemed to have been acted out by two different people. But now it was brought back abruptly, helped along by his insufferable attitude of righteousness. He seemed quite under the impression that it was she who owed him some sort of gratitude for being rescued from the undesirable company of Mike Costello.

Her anger and resentment came back with force. "Not even a country girl like me would be so naive as to expect an apology from the infallible Mr. Hawker," she told him with a disparaging twist of the lips.

"I'm glad to hear it," he returned, and looked at her intensely for a moment before adding, "for there is nothing tonight that I have regretted."

His meaning was clear, and her mind flashing back to his kiss, she looked away in alarm. He grinned and said, "Don't forget what I told you . . . about that extra lock."

She nodded mutely.

"Good night, Sally," he called lightly before turning toward the stairs. It was the first time he had used her name and this small intimacy, like so many of his other actions tonight, caught her unawares and added to her mounting confusion.

Silently she closed the door and leaned against it for a long moment. This night had seemed like an eternity. Was it only a few hours ago that she was in this room getting ready to go out with Mike? Where was Mike now, and what was he thinking? she wondered, but did not linger on the thought. Her mind was too full of other things, so puzzling, so disconcerting that she spent the better part of the night tossing in her bed, trying to make sense out of them.

CHAPTER SEVEN

"Miss Beecham left a message for you," Myrna Martin announced importantly one morning when Sally arrived at the office. "She wants you to meet her at the Waldorf-Astoria for that charity fashion showing tonight. You are to meet her in the lobby at eight."

Sally sighed impatiently. She didn't know which was worse—the tedium of sitting around the social department with almost nothing to do, or these nightly summonses to Althea's side to run unnecessary errands for her. The social reporter had gotten along very well without an assistant before, the help of her secretary being more than adequate. But now that she had one, she made the best use of the situation to enlarge her own importance before her friends. She would order Sally to wait on her at one of her functions

on the smallest of excuses, sometimes for no more
reason than to give her a few names on a guest list
which she could easily have telephoned to the ever-
eager Miss Martin.

Sally longed to be back in the atmosphere of the
city room, absorbing the daily excitement the newspaper generated, sharing in the gossip and flow of
newspaper talk with the other reporters, but pride
kept her out of the city room. She never went in
there, though the other reporters, noisily sympathetic,
sometimes came to visit her and brought her up to
date on everything that was happening.

Once, to her great surprise, Bill McIntire popped
in to ask how she was doing. He was self-conscious
and uncomfortable, and fidgeted restlessly the whole
time he was there, looking as much at ease in the
social department as the proverbial bull in the china
shop. Sally was gratified and cheered by his unexpected visit.

Miss Martin viewed all these outside intrusions with
the stern-lipped suspicion of a jailer who was keeping
an eye on everything so she could make a faithful
report to the warden afterward. Sally was quite sure
her every move was reported to Althea.

After that strange evening at the Chantilly Room,
she had seen very little of Mike. At first she was apprehensive about meeting him, being every bit as embarrassed about what had happened as she imagined
he would be. She did not enjoy seeing anyone humiliated and even felt a little ashamed for the contempt
she now felt for him. But she had apparently overesti-
mated Mike's sensitivity and underestimated his ability to bounce back.

"Hello, gorgeous," he greeted her winningly the
first time they met after the incident, in the office
corridor.

"How are you, Mike?" she answered brightly, but
her eyes were reluctant to meet his.

For a few minutes he chatted on as if nothing

regrettable had happened between them, and she was torn between relief and an even stronger sense of contempt for him. He did not allude to the disastrous evening, or mention Hawker's name, and from this she knew that at least he was as anxious to ignore what had passed as she was to forget it.

After that she saw him only in passing; he didn't try to contact her at home. She had expected some explanation, some sort of apology for his ungallant behavior, but he had given none. Now she was grateful that he seemed anxious to avoid her.

The weather had turned from suffocating summer heat to an autumn crispness, and Sally enjoyed the unusually clear air over Manhattan as she walked down Park Avenue toward the Waldorf. She remembered with a twinge of nostalgia how invigorating this time of year was in Glenbrook, how the countryside smelled and looked with the turning of the leaves. So far she hadn't had enough time off to pay a visit home, though she spoke with her aunt and uncle frequently. She remembered with a surge of joy that she would be back at the Holloway home for Thanksgiving, having been promised a few days vacation.

She turned into the lobby of the Waldorf promptly at eight, but as usual, Althea kept her waiting. Sally moved to a quiet corner, watching the passing parade of well-dressed people with little interest.

It was more than a half hour before Althea emerged from one of the reception rooms and came toward her. In public, her attitude was always a little vague and condescending, as if Sally were so insignificant that she had almost forgotten about her. Usually she was surrounded by a group of friends who all seemed to be feigning boredom with everything around them. Sally, much to Althea's chagrin, refused to be intimidated and was quite unimpressed by the social columnist's distinguished clique.

As she patiently listened to Althea's quite unnecessary instructions, she heard a soft voice beside her.

"It's . . . Miss Spencer, isn't it?" Turning, Sally found herself face to face with Michelle Campbell-Jones. A genuinely glad smile lit up that exquisite face as she shook hands with the young reporter.

"I'm very pleased to meet you again. How have you been?" she inquired in her well-bred voice.

"Very well," Sally replied smiling. "But more importantly, how have things been working out for you?"

"Well," the girl began, then her eyes seemed to notice Althea for the first time. She had been standing there, looking with unbecoming amazement from Sally to the other girl, not quite able to believe that they knew each other in such a friendly way. Being a terrible snob, she regarded Miss Campbell-Jones, who was out of her own social and financial league, with due deference. She was puzzled by the seeming intimacy between her assistant and the heiress.

"Miss Beecham, we have a few things to talk over. You don't mind, do you?" she asked with just a hint of dismissal. Then drawing her arm through Sally's, she led her out of earshot.

"Don't tell me you are working with her?" she asked, shooting a look of distaste in Althea's direction.

"Yes, I am, but that's a long story," Sally sighed. "I'd much rather hear your news first."

"Things are going wonderfully for us," Miss Campbell-Jones whispered, her eyes radiant. "The divorce is almost final now and so far it hasn't leaked to the papers, thanks to you. Marc plans to make a simple announcement when it is all over. Of course," she added earnestly, "you will be the first to know everything. I . . . that is, we, are most grateful to you."

They chatted for a while longer, then the conversation turned to Sally. The other girl was distressed to hear the brief account of what had happened as a result of her concealment of that sensational story.

"But that is just dreadful," she said with concern. "I'm so sorry to hear you got into trouble for protecting us. Really, it's awful," she repeated with another look of displeasure in Althea's direction.

Sally dismissed her consternation with a wave of her hand. "Don't worry about me," she assured her. "All I need is one really good story and I'll be back in good graces again."

"I'll see what I can do about that," Michelle Campbell-Jones said thoughtfully, and she was still a little preoccupied when they parted.

Althea lost no time in getting to Sally's side. "You seem to have the knack of making yourself noticed by the right people," she commented sourly, with not a little envy in her voice.

"And the wrong," Sally amended in an undertone, but Althea had not heard.

"How long have you been so friendly with Michelle Campbell-Jones?" Althea asked, unable to hide her keen curiosity.

"Not very long at all," Sally replied with enough vagueness to annoy the other woman. She wasn't going to satisfy her rude curiosity. Let her fret over her high connections all night if she wished.

Althea shrugged angrily and curtly dismissed her. Sally, thankful to be gone, left the hotel with alacrity and decided to walk over to the Globe Building.

These irregular hours did not give her much chance to go out at night. She was at Althea's beck and call constantly and never knew what the woman's whim would demand of her next. But she did not have much desire for company these days, anyway. Since that incident with Mike and Hawker a month ago, she had been unable to shake off a strange mood of depression and preferred to be alone with her thoughts most of the time.

When she did have the time off, she wandered all over Manhattan by herself. She visited museums, went to art exhibits, attended concerts, or just strolled along the busy, exciting streets of the most lively city in the world. On several warm nights she caught the Staten Island ferry for a round trip because she loved the view of Manhattan the ride afforded. And occasionally she had dinner with Cathy and Margaret or went to a movie with them when the girls were off duty from their nursing, but these times were infrequent because the girls worked irregular hours, too.

Sally had fought hard to keep her mind off Rafe Hawker and to dispell the perplexing mixture of emotions he provoked in her, but his memory persisted in haunting her whether she was at work in his building or at home in the apartment where his presence somehow still lingered.

Back at her apartment, after she completed work that night, she paced about restlessly. Her eyes sought the now barely visible spot on the rug where the coffee had been spilled. Involuntarily, she had glanced there a hundred times since it had happened and it never failed to arouse conflicting feelings in her.

Had that really been Rafe Hawker sitting there listening raptly to her tales of her family? Had it been those strong, wiry hands that had touched her so gently, those firm lips that had caressed her so tenderly? She shook her head, unable to reconcile those gestures with the other Rafe Hawker she knew, the one who had destroyed her evening out with Mike Costello with such arrogance, afterward telling her he was pleased with himself for doing so. Or the one who was punishing her in that ridiculous and humiliating job, no doubt to amuse his girl friend.

As always, the thought of Althea immediately restored her anger to its peak. She had not seen them together since that evening at the theatre; indeed, she had not seen Hawker since her own fateful night with him and she had no doubt that Althea would never again bring her along to a function that Hawker was likely to attend. It was almost inconceivable that the disdainful publisher could be interested in a woman like Althea, she mused. Yet in all evidence, he was.

Certainly, Althea would show a very different side of herself to him than she allowed Sally to see. Possibly she kept her ill temper and off-putting greed in check when she was in his company. But surely a man of his penetrating discernment could see through Althea's flimsy act. But maybe not, Sally shrugged, maybe he was like so many other men whose vanity was easily satisfied by a beautiful woman. In any case, everything she had seen and heard pointed to the unalterable fact that he was seeing a great deal of Althea.

They were welcome to each other, she told herself, resolving for the hundredth time not to care.

"It's Mr. Hawker on the line for you, Miss Beecham," Myrna Martin croaked, her voice almost failing her in her excitement.

For once Althea dropped her pretended air of boredom and hurried into her office, closing the door behind her.

And for once Sally was not amused by Miss Martin's frenzy of excitement brought on by the phone call; she was too busy nursing a growing misery inside her. She sat numbly at her desk, trying to concentrate and barely controlling an urge to rush out of the room. What a state of confusion I'm in, she scolded herself angrily. One minute I'm full of anger for something he has said or done, heartily wishing never to cross his path again, and the next minute I'm reduced to depression because he's making a date with his girl friend. If only I could be back in the city room absorbed in some serious work, out of earshot of everything that was happening between him and Althea.

The door opened a little while later and Althea came out smiling smugly.

"You need not stay around for the rest of the day," she said as she turned carelessly to Sally. "I don't think there's anything left that Miss Martin and I cannot attend to. You might as well go home now."

Sally could not hide her surprise at such unaccustomed magnanimity. "But it's only three o'clock," she said with a glance at her watch. Even when there was nothing for her to do and time lagged emptily, she was never offered the afternoon off.

"That doesn't matter." Althea waved impatiently.

"There is no point in you staying. You may go." She sounded abrupt, as if she was most anxious for Sally to be gone.

Sally shrugged and gathered her things together. She was not convinced that Althea had had a sudden impulse to be generous, and suspected she had some other motive for dismissing her for the afternoon. "Okay, then, I'm off," she said. "I'll see you tomorrow."

She thought she heard a sigh of relief after Althea's good-bye.

Walking toward the elevator, she ran into Bill McIntire. "I've had a hell of a day," he replied to her inquiries with an exhausted sigh.

On impulse Sally ventured, "I've been given the rest of the afternoon off. Why don't you let me buy you a drink to restore your sanity?"

To her surprise the city editor accepted the invitation eagerly. "The best break I've had today," he grinned. "For once I'm glad to leave this place."

Sally waited while he collected his coat and briefcase, and the two of them left the building, walking the short distance to The Headliner. The bar was jammed with drinkers from *The Globe* even at this hour of the afternoon. Among them, Sally noted with displeasure, was Mike Costello.

She returned his loud greeting with a wave, then purposefully turned her back on him, sitting down on a bar stool opposite Bill McIntire. She rarely came to this bar, but whenever she did she enjoyed its boisterous atmosphere and submerged herself readily in all the newspaper chatter.

It was not long before she was deep in conversation with the city editor, telling him of her start-in *The Patriot* and of its editor Cornelius Smith. He in turn told her about his early newspaper years.

He had started on *The Globe* long before Rafe Hawker bought it and became its publisher, so he had seen a lot of changes in his time. For Hawker he had an almost worshipful regard. He told Sally he admired him for his quick understanding of newspapers and his shrewd talent for making them sell.

Relaxed by her company and a couple of drinks, he talked with uncharacteristic animation of some of the Hawker exploits he had witnessed. The more outrageous and daring they were, the more admiringly he talked of them. A newspaperman through and through, he judged the publisher on a strictly professional level. The private man, he admitted, was a mystery even to him, although he was probably closer to him on the paper than anyone else, having worked with him side by side to pull *The Globe* back from bankruptcy.

"You can only get to within a certain distance of Rafe Hawker and no further," he mused, shaking his head. "There seems to be a barricade built around the inner man that no one to my knowledge has ever penetrated. From what little I know of him, I suspect it's a protective barrier. I know for certain that Hawker had been through some pretty rough times before he got to where he is today."

Sally listened with fascination, eager to learn a little more about the man who had been so much in her thoughts lately. She was deeply interested in everything the usually reserved Bill McIntire was telling her, and they were deeply absorbed in their conversation when an unwelcome voice broke in.

"Stealing my girl, McIntire?" Mike Costello boomed. With a sense of dread, Sally noticed that he was more than slightly drunk. Mike tended to overindulge, though in her company he carefully watched how much he drank.

Now his face was flushed and his voice overloud. Sally winced at his "my girl" and Bill McIntire's face was turning stony.

"Hello, Costello," he muttered without enthusiasm. He was a forthright man who made no secret of the fact that he had little time for the paper's star columnist, who in his opinion was something of a prima donna.

"I've got to talk to you, Sal," Mike said, weaving unsteadily.

Bill McIntire downed his drink quickly and gathered his things. "I've got to run anyway. See you soon . . . in the city room, I hope." With a wink at her and a grudging nod at Mike he was gone.

She was more than a little annoyed at Mike for interrupting a perfectly pleasant conversation and had no wish to hear anything he had to say. She made a move to go but he had already fastened his hand on her shoulder. With a show of patience, she looked at him.

"What is it, Mike?"

"You know what it is." There was a pleading note in his voice and a sad look in his eyes.

"I don't have either the time or inclination to play guessing games or talk in riddles," she answered, her patience breaking. "Out with it, Mike."

"You've been avoiding me like poison these last few weeks," he said accusingly. "I want to know why."

Sally looked at him with disbelief. Just how shamelessly thick skinned was the man?

Mike shifted his eyes uneasily. "If it's about that night I took you to dinner . . . you can hardly blame me for what happened." His laugh was sheepish.

Sally continued staring at him for a long moment during which he had the grace to look embarrassed. "I don't blame you," she said quietly and, unable to look at him any longer, turned away.

Immediately Mike was on the defensive. "What was I supposed to do? It was partly your fault you know. You keep denying that there's anything between you yet you could see how jealous Hawker was that night. I felt caught in the middle." He tried a nervous laugh, but when Sally kept her head averted, his voice rose to a whine. "What was I supposed to do? Make a scene? I thought the decent thing to do was to act civilized and leave quietly."

His voice was rising steadily, Sally realized with

embarrassment. It was beginning to dominate the conversation around them. She sensed that people nearby had gone quiet, and a tangible hush was spreading across the bar. She looked up suddenly and saw that their attention was not directed at Mike. It was riveted in the other direction where Rafe Hawker was making his way toward them.

Hawker's appearance caused a nervous ripple throughout the room. Never before had the publisher of *The Globe* come to the bar where most of his reporters spent so much of their free time. Those who should have been at their typewriters tried to shrink out of sight, but Hawker ignored everyone as he stopped beside Sally.

"I was told I might find you here. Little early for you to be drinking, isn't it?" His voice was low so that only she could hear but there was a biting edge to it.

The murmur of conversation started up again in an attempt to make things appear normal. Her first reaction of complete amazement at his appearance there was overtaken by anger at his immediate attack. Mike Costello remained standing at her side, completely ignored by Hawker. He had not given him so much as a glance.

"Are you checking up on me, sir?" Sally's lips set tightly.

"It so happens I am. Not unreasonable of me during working hours, would you agree?" he returned with chilling sarcasm. "At least I see you can hold your liquor better than your boyfriend."

Sally's first impulse was to storm out of there, but the threatening look in his eyes warned her that he would not let her get away easily. She closed her eyes for a fraction of a second to get her anger under control. When she opened them again, she saw with a measure of relief that someone had had the sense to hustle the very drunk Mike away. The two of them remained staring stonily at each other.

"Well?" Hawker demanded roughly.

"Well nothing," she replied in a voice trembling with anger. "If you are expecting an explanation, you are wasting your time. You never ask questions first, do you? You open a conversation by accusing."

People all around were looking at them with covert curiosity but she was oblivious to everything but her rising anger and need to lash out at him.

"I'll come clean if you like," she began with an almost calm fury. Her face had paled in a tightly drawn mask, making her eyes look huge and her clenched fists showed white at the knuckles.

"I come here all the time. I sneak out of work whenever I can to consume great quantities of liquor." Despite a dangerous flicker in Hawker's eyes, she continued recklessly. "I'm *The Globe*'s resident lush. Sometimes I'm here waiting at the door before opening time, and most nights they have to throw me out long after closing. You've caught me in the act, Mr. Hawker. Now you can fire me again."

She made a move to rise, but the expression on Hawker's face told her he wouldn't let her leave just yet.

"Just one minute." His voice was quietly threatening. "Why this sudden indignation? I go down to your office to be told that you have disappeared for the afternoon, and no one knows where. Then I'm informed you are most likely to be found at your regular hangout—this bar. Sure enough, I come here to find you, once more in the company of that drunken, self-important bum, Mike Costello, and you accuse me of jumping to conclusions?"

The color returned to Sally's cheeks with full force at this piece of treachery by Althea. She had no doubt now that Althea had known Hawker was coming down to their office; he had probably told her so in the phone call, and that was why she had been so anxious to get rid of her. But then to lie so viciously and tell him she had disappeared without explanation during working hours! This seemed to be an open declaration of war from Althea.

"I don't suppose your 'informer,'" she countered with bitter emphasis on the word, "told you that she gave me the afternoon off? In fact she practically hustled me out of the office."

A light dawned in Hawker's eyes, but he asked with undiminished coldness, "And this is how you chose to spend it?"

Sally knew she could have told him then that she rarely came here, that she had made an exception this afternoon to have a drink with Bill McIntire. But she would make no excuses to him. Let him think what he liked. But why had he come to seek her out? His expression was closed, discouraging, and she could discern nothing from it.

I've certainly made a fine spectacle of myself this afternoon, Sally thought with exasperation. First it was Mike Costello's loud voice that had attracted attention to her; now it was the uncalled-for honor of Mr. Hawker's company. "I want to leave now," she murmured hastily.

"I think it's time you did," he agreed.

Once on the street Sally paused, wondering if he would tell her why he had been looking for her, though she kept her head angrily averted.

Interpreting her hesitancy correctly, he said in a brittle voice, "There *was* something I wanted to talk to you about, but it doesn't matter now."

Despite all that had gone before, she felt a keen disappointment and her curiosity increased. For a moment she was tempted again to explain, but the sight of his relentless expression deterred her. He had obviously already made up his mind about her—once again without giving her the benefit of the doubt—and there was no point in trying to change it.

Angry as Sally was, she felt stricken by Hawker's cold regard. She had not seen him in over a month, and in that time, dwelling on the memory of their last meeting, she had allowed herself some foolish fancies about him, dreams that lay shattered now under his impersonal glance.

Afraid of his uncanny ability to read her mind, she blurted a hasty farewell and walked abruptly away. If he responded she did not hear it, and he made no attempt to restrain or follow her. She walked the blocks to her apartment in a self-imposed trance.

It was not until she had closed her door behind her that she allowed the thoughts to come back to her. As usual after a meeting with him, they were painfully confused and it was this confusion that she most resented about him. If she could once and for all make up her mind that he was heartless and arrogant, almost to the point of being sadistic, then she could always be on her guard and much less vulnerable to his attacks. But whenever a softer look stole into those granite eyes or his voice lost its frosty edge, she was at once disarmed, totally disconcerted by the contradictions in his character.

Never before in her life had Sally known such inner turbulence. Of course, she had had romantic misunderstandings which had caused her momentary pain, but she had always prided herself on her sensibility.

Above her bed in Glenbrook hung her favorite motto: "Starve the imagination and feed the will." She had taken this piece of wisdom to heart and it had helped her avoid many an unhappy experience. Perhaps she should have brought it with her from home and placed it in a position of prominence, she thought ruefully. It was because she had let her imagination stray and dwell on daydreams that she now found herself unable to control her emotions. What a changed person she had become since she left home. Was it only such a short time ago?

The thought of home made her yearn for the comfort, the ordinary, uncomplicated love of her family. She reached for the telephone and dialed her Aunt Emily's number.

* * *

Wearily, the next day, Sally let herself into her apartment and, kicking her shoes off, sank down on her bed in the sleeping alcove. She closed her eyes and felt the frustrations of the day course through her body.

Despite her resolve not to lose her temper, she had had a showdown with Althea that day. As soon as the social writer had come into the office, Sally had followed her into her room and closed the door behind them with a resounding slam.

With barely controlled anger Sally confronted Althea with all her treachery of the day before, when she had deliberately lied to Rafe Hawker to cause trouble for her. Succinctly, she told Althea what she thought of her character and many other things that had built up inside her over the past couple of months.

From her devastated expression it was clear that no one had ever spoken to Althea like that before. She stared at Sally, her eyes reduced to piercing slits, and it was a while before she managed to gasp, "How *dare* you! Are you aware of my position here? Of who I *am?*"

"Yes, Althea, I am painfully aware of that," Sally returned, keeping her voice even with great effort. "Probably the most devious, conceited, and unpleasant person I have ever had the misfortune to come in contact with."

Althea's cold blue eyes dilated with shock as she exclaimed, "I think you are forgetting your place!"

"No, I think you are exaggerating the importance of your own, Althea. You seem to be under the impression that your position entitles you to tell damaging lies without having to take the consequences. I have catered to your vanity for weeks now by serving your whims without complaint. But I warn you, I'm not prepared to tolerate your dishonesty as well."

Ignoring Althea's outraged exclamations, she strolled to the door, turning with her hand on the knob. "You might like to know that when you tried to do me harm yesterday you managed to do yourself some as well. I had opportunity to set Mr. Hawker right about some of the facts. Perhaps now he knows you for the liar you are."

As she lay tiredly on her bed, Sally realized with dismay that her position in the social department would be an impossible one from now on. It was tolerable only as long as she had been prepared to put up with Althea's behavior. Now that she had openly called the woman a liar, she knew her days were numbered. She doubted that Althea would dare to complain to Hawker after this particular incident. After all, she *had* been caught in a lie. But she would find a way somehow of getting rid of her. Of that Sally was certain.

Her thoughts were interrupted by the telephone and she let its shrill ring continue for a moment, tempted not to answer it. But it could be one of her family, she reasoned, and reached for the receiver.

"Hello, Miss Spencer?" the voice asked tentatively. She recognized it immediately and anticipation shot through her.

"Miss Campbell-Jones, how are you?" she returned eagerly.

"I'm so glad to find you at home," the soft voice said with relief. "I've been trying to contact you at your office, but you were out most of the afternoon." Her voice rose a little with excitement. "I . . . that is, *we*, think we might have a good story for you."

Instantly all weariness left Sally, an alertness taking its place. She subdued her own excitement as she told the other girl, "That's wonderful news and couldn't come at a better time. Just tell me what it is and I'll get right to it."

"Well, it's not something I can go into over the telephone," the other girl laughed with embarrassment, "but if you could spare the time to meet Marc and me in about a half-hour, I think you would find the trouble worth your while. Please come alone," she added in a worried tone. "No one but you can be in on this."

After taking down the exclusive East Side address, Sally made a dash for the bathroom. She had just time enough for the quickest of showers to wash away the last traces of tiredness that hadn't been expelled by her excitement. She was refreshed and dry in less than five minutes and decided to change from the skirt and pullover she had been wearing during the day. Given the impressive address and the lateness of the day, she thought she had better be prepared in a dress that was a little more formal.

She slipped into a brown silk jersey dress that was both simple and elegant and decided on her single strand of baroque pearls for a touch of decoration. A few dabs of makeup and a few strokes with the brush, and ten minutes later she was out the door, spraying perfume behind her ears as she dashed down the stairs.

She managed to secure a cab right away and, sitting back, she had time at last to speculate on the reason for Michelle Campbell-Jones's mysterious call.

The woman had promised her a good story and Sally was confident she would get one, knowing that since the heiress was rarely available to the press, any story involving her would be welcomed by *The Globe*. Perhaps the interview would be with Marc Whitfield, involving a Washington exclusive, which would be equally well received by the paper. Sally's blood raced with impatience; she was barely able to sit still during the short ride. Through her mind kept running the thought that this could be her salvation, her means of getting back into the city room and back to real reporting at last.

The cab dropped her outside an elegant town house in the Sutton Place neighborhood. It was already dusk and Sally glimpsed massive chandeliers alight behind dark woven drapes on the first floor.

Her ring was answered by a uniformed maid who, after politely taking her name, ushered her into a large

salon opening from the hall. Sally's first glimpse at the
small group of people in the room made her thankful
for her foresight in having changed her dress. There
were three distinguished-looking men and a beautifully groomed woman standing with drinks in their
hands by an ornate marble fireplace. She recognized
Marc Whitfield coming toward her, his hands out-
stretched, a welcoming smile on his face.

"So pleased to see you again, Miss Spencer. I hope
at last we will be able to repay you for your kindness."

Before Sally could venture a question, he was introducing her to the others in the room. The elegantly
groomed woman and one of the men by her side were
the host and hostess, owners of the house and long-
time friends of the senator. The other, older gentleman
was a judge, his name well known to Sally. They all
showed a friendly politeness toward her, but Sally was
still puzzling over her reason for being there when
Michelle Campbell-Jones entered the room.

A general murmur of admiration went up at the
sight of her, and Marc Whitfield glanced with open
adoration at the lovely vision she created. Sally thought
she had never seen anyone so beautiful.

The heiress came toward them a little shyly, dressed
in a floor-length cream dress of exquisitely delicate
lace falling softly about her tall, slim body. Her raven
black hair was dressed in a simple style, falling to her
shoulders with an old-fashioned and very beautiful
coronet of white roses and gardenias circling the crown
of her head. She held a matching bouquet and wore
no jewelry except for a diamond engagement ring that
flashed dazzlingly on her finger.

Her smiling dark eyes met Sally's and she was sure
then of what her exclusive story was to be. She smiled
back at the bride joyously.

"Thanks to you, Sally, we are able to do this without the hysteria and chaos that would have followed
had you let our secret out in your story," Marc Whitfield explained. "Michelle told me that you got into

hot water because of your kind consideration for us, and we decided the best way to get you out of it was to invite you to our wedding. We meant to keep it a secret until after it was over, with just our friends here present, but as Michelle pointed out to me, you too have become a friend."

"Not even our families know yet, so it really will be an exclusive for you," the bride added.

At that moment, looking at the couple's unmistakable happiness, Sally thought that everything that had happened to her, all the misery she had been put through, was worth it, just to be able to be witness to this scene.

During the brief but intimate ceremony performed by the judge, she forgot that she was getting an exclusive news story and for a while knew only that she was part of a very joyous moment in the lives of two people who were totally in love. That they also happened to be wealthy and famous did not matter then. The whole affair was carried out with a quiet dignity which Sally thought a lot of more elaborate weddings sadly lacked.

When the vows had been exchanged, toasts were proposed and, afterward, the hostess led them to the dining hall where the table was laid for dinner. She insisted that Sally stay for the meal and the bride joined in her entreaties.

"Otherwise who shall I throw my bouquet to?" she smiled.

Throughout dinner the conversation flowed freely on a great number of subjects, and Sally, who an hour ago had not known three of the people and had met the other two only briefly, found herself fitting in with ease. Only once, when the judge who was seated beside her asked, "What is that rascal Rafe Hawker really like?" was her happy mood dispelled a bit.

"I don't know," she replied with honesty. "I don't think anyone really does."

The others all appeared to be fascinated by the man and joined in the questioning.

"Have you ever met him? Is he as striking looking as in his pictures?" the hostess wanted to know.

"Yes, I've met him and he is . . . very striking looking," Sally answered, her face flushing slightly at a treacherous memory. "But to meet him, even to work closely with him, does not mean knowing him."

The conversation revolved around the publisher for a while longer and Sally felt an unexpected urge to defend him whenever one of the party brought up some criticism of him.

After dinner, the host took some pictures of the newlyweds. They were planning to take a private plane to their honeymoon destination but Sally was too discreet to ask where. It was enough that she had the story of their clandestine wedding; it would be too much if the press was to hound them during their honeymoon, too.

After another drink, she thanked her host and hostess and shook hands with the judge, who seemed to be rather taken with her. As she took her leave of the young couple, she gave them her genuine good wishes and expressed her gratitude for the story they had given her.

The bride walked to the door with her and Sally said, "Good-bye for now Miss Camp— Oh, no, it's Mrs. Whitfield now, isn't it?" she corrected, laughing.

"Yes, but I would much rather you called me Michelle. Would you?"

The parting between the two young women was warm. From their short acquaintance an understanding and great liking had grown between them.

When Sally was at the gate, the other girl called after her.

"Sally, I almost forgot. Wait just a moment." She disappeared into the house and reappeared a few moments later.

"Here," she called gaily, and the bridal bouquet

came sailing at Sally. She caught it deftly. "Don't forget to invite me when it's your turn," Michelle called after her.

Sally spent the short taxi drive to *The Globe* with her nose pressed dreamily into the fragrant flowers. Their heady smell started a sweet pain stirring somewhere in a secret place within her. It was not the first bridal bouquet that had been thrown deliberately in her direction. As her girl friends were married one by one, after they left school, they pointedly aimed their wedding bouquets at her with good-natured hints about her following in their footsteps down the isle. But this was the first time she had felt more than amusement at catching one. She wasn't sure what had brought on the suddenly sentimental mood that took hold of her, but she was beginning to suspect.

When she saw the brightly lit Globe Building before her, all her thoughts concentrated on one subject: her story. Her heart beat with familiar excitement as, getting out on the tenth floor, she took the turn toward the city room instead of the social department as she had done for so many unhappy weeks.

Most of the staff had long gone, and would not be in again until the early hours of the morning when, with dawn, the paper started coming to life. There were a few people on night duty throughout the room, all strangers to Sally, and no one looked up as she took a seat at one of the vacant desks and picked up the telephone. She asked the switchboard to put her through to Bill McIntire's home number.

"Hello?" the abrupt voice barked.

"Mr. McIntire, this is Sally Spencer. I'm sorry to bother you at home but I think I have a story you would want to know about. I've just come from the wedding of Michelle Campbell-Jones and Senator Marc Whitfield."

There was a pause at the other end and then the city editor's brusque voice, tinged with excitement, demanded, "Has anyone else got the story?"

"No, I have it exclusively," she told him.

"Start writing it at once and call me when you've finished. Meanwhile, put me on to the night news editor." It was typical of Bill McIntire that he neither wasted time in wondering how she had gotten the story or in congratulating her for it. His first instinct was always to get it down on paper as quickly as possible.

Sally was aware of the excitement the story had generated when the night news editor came over every few minutes to hover anxiously, peering at her copy over her shoulder. She typed rapidly, words spilling smoothly onto paper. It was a straightforward, sensational news story, embellished for the sake of *The Globe*'s fashion-conscious readers with details of how the bride had looked, what she had worn, the furnishings in the room where the couple were married, and all other details that tantalized the readership. However, she balked at taking it to excess and recounted the wedding with as much subdued enthusiasm as she thought would satisfy the editors.

She had been given a roll of film of the wedding by the host, and the photo and art departments were already working on it.

Her story completed, she rang the city editor.

"I've had a copyboy read it to me over the phone," he told her. "Sounds like excellent stuff. Unless New York is bombed overnight, or someone makes an attempt on the President, you've got yourself tomorrow's front-page story. I guess we'll be seeing you back in the city room now," he added gruffly, but Sally detected the note of satisfaction in his voice.

That night she went home in a happier frame of mind than she had been in for a long time. The future was looking bright again.

CHAPTER EIGHT

"It's for you," Miss Martin announced with an ungracious sniff, handing Sally the telephone.

"Eve Tarrant here," the cheerful voice on the other end said. "Come on up, honey, Mr. Hawker would like to see you."

Sally chided herself for the betraying plunge her stomach took at the sound of his name and in the elevator noticed with dismay that her hands were not quite steady and her throat felt painfully dry. She was almost certain the summons to the publisher's office was the result of her front-page story the previous day, but with Rafe Hawker one could never know for sure. It was just as likely that she had displeased him again in some mysterious way she did not even suspect yet. In any case, whatever turn his mood took, she would be prepared.

When she stepped out of the elevator into the handsome lobby, she took in a long steadying pull of cool air, and smoothed down her hair in an unconscious nervous gesture.

"How have you been, honey?" Mrs. Tarrant asked heartily when Sally was ushered into her office by one of the secretaries in the outer room. She found the woman's unpretentious cheeriness a welcome, steadying effect.

"Just fine, thank you, Mrs. Tarrant," she smiled back.

"And you look it, too," the woman returned, brushing an approving glance over Sally's golden-haloed head and slim figure in a simple cornflower blue skirt-and-sweater outfit of fine cashmere wool. "Just one moment and I'll buzz Mr. Hawker to tell him you are here."

Then Sally was once more stepping through those massive doors into his quietly luxurious office. Rafe Hawker was standing by one of the bookcases, absorbed in reading something, and he instructed her without turning around.

"Please sit down, Miss Spencer. I'll be with you in a moment."

Sally obeyed, choosing a chair at some distance from his desk, and took the opportunity to look at the room more closely than she had had time to do on her previous visit.

From under her lashes, safe in the knowledge that his attention was engaged elsewhere, she looked at him closely. It wasn't often that she had the chance to look at him so freely, without having to parry one of his own disturbing looks. She took in the high forehead, the charcoal-gray eyebrows shielding his piercing eyes, the strong straight nose, the straight mouth drawn into a line. "Is he really so striking looking?" her hostess at the wedding had asked her. Yes, she agreed silently to herself, definitely one of the most striking-looking men she had ever seen.

From the face that held controlled calm, as if long ago he had imposed his steel will over his emotions, her eyes traveled to his strong lean hands with their extraordinarily long fingers . . . the same fingers that had once—a lifetime ago—caressed her neck. His clothes, as always, were immaculate and rather conservative. She could not imagine him ever wearing anything flamboyant. His perfectly tailored suits like his perfectly furnished office gave nothing away of the inner man.

In one swift move Hawker had swung around and turned his eyes on her. They had the effect of powerful searchlights suddenly switched on her, catching her, as always, unawares. Hawker seemed to know that she had been furtively looking at him and his eyes reflected amusement. He settled back in his chair as if preparing to enjoy himself and said to her with a wry smile, "I see you have chosen the farthest chair possible, Miss Spencer. Shall I move mine up to that end of the room or would you like to join me?"

"I was afraid you might accuse me of eavesdropping if I sat any closer, sir," Sally replied pertly, choosing a chair nearer to his desk. She was determined to hold her own this time, no matter what. If he chose to open the conversation with sarcasm, so be it.

"No, I noticed you were not eavesdropping," he agreed. "You were too busy sizing me up from under those long lashes. What did you decide?"

With effort she returned his look boldly. "Nothing new, just confirming something I had already decided some time ago."

"So you have given me some thought before," he said, smiling. "How did you find me?"

Sally felt with panic that the conversation was taking a dangerous turn, at least dangerous to herself. "I won't ask you what you think of me and I won't tell you my opinion of you in return," she replied a little stiffly.

"Just as well," he agreed coolly and added with deliberation, "I think I would come out the loser in that exchange."

She felt a familiar confusion at his unexpected remarks and wanted desperately to put an end to this exchange. Surely he had not called her to his office to practice verbal volleys with her.

"What was it you wanted to see me about, Mr. Hawker?" she asked with emphasis.

"Oh yes, that," he said negligently, shifting his intense gaze. "Well, of course, it is about your story yesterday. It was quite a scoop, for both you and the paper. I won't ask how you came by it; it's a reporter's privilege to keep her sources secret. I suppose you are anxious to be reinstated in the city room?"

"Yes, I would like that very much," she replied, trying to subdue her eagerness.

Hawker regarded her with some amusement. "Are you sure you won't mind leaving the social department?"

"Very sure," she replied, ignoring his teasing tone.

His eyebrows shot up in mock surprise and he shook his head. "I would have thought you would be reluctant to part with your good friends there."

If he wished to amuse himself at her expense she would not gratify him by taking the bait, she decided, looking back at him steadily. No doubt he had by now become fully aware of the animosity between her and Althea, which was all the more reason for her not to be drawn into a discussion on this subject. She could not help wondering how much malicious gossip Althea had fed him. Knowing her venomous nature, the possibilities were endless.

"And what would you do if I still insisted that you stay on as Miss Beecham's assistant?"

The possibility came as a jarring shock to Sally, and she was instantly angered. "I would consider you most unjust and resign at once," she replied with flashing eyes.

"No wonder you have such a lovely complexion," he remarked irrelevantly. "You're either blushing with anger and indignation or out of maidenly embarrassment."

Sally's hands involuntarily flew to her cheeks and his smile broadened. "Both are very becoming reasons, I assure you . . . and good for the circulation." So she had fallen into his trap after all by losing her temper at the suggestion that she stay on with Althea, not realizing that he had only been teasing her.

"You need not worry," he continued, reading her thoughts. "You shall have your rightful place back in the city room. I was only curious to see how far you would go if you were crossed. Now I know."

He was softly laughing at her but somehow it didn't matter. Her punishment and exile were over and she had endured them without a single complaint to him. Once more she would be back on the job she loved more than anything else, away from the degrading tedium of the social department and Althea. Yes, above all Althea. She would be able to close her mind to everything but her work. She would concentrate on it completely and block out all those foolish notions that had been undermining her peace of mind in the past few weeks.

Simply, she said to him, "Thank you."

For a long moment Hawker sat with his head slightly bowed, staring unseeingly at the desk before him, his brow creased in a frown. She sensed that he was turning something over in his mind and had the strange feeling that he was on the verge of saying or asking something that had nothing to do with the subject under discussion.

The moment passed and he looked up abruptly, his eyes meeting hers. Whatever emotion had passed through him was now replaced by his customary mask of calculated control. He had obviously changed his mind about whatever he was about to say, and she was reminded of the last time when he had done the same thing outside The Headliner. Again she felt the keen disappointment.

She rose to leave and Hawker stood up with her. "By the way," he said, and her heart beat with fresh anticipation. "Have you had that extra lock fitted to your door yet?"

She felt a letdown as she shook her head. A security lock had been the furthest thing from her mind that moment.

"Well, you had better do so," he advised. "I've warned you about the necessity for security in that apartment." She was warmly gratified at his concern, but his next words managed to destroy all that.

"Just another word of advice, Miss Spencer. If you are thinking of celebrating your return to the newsroom, don't do it with Mike Costello." At the quick flash of resentment in her eyes, he added in a tone of insolence, "I have a feeling he is not the type of man your Aunt Emily would approve of."

Sally refused to let him see her sweeping anger and left the room without another word.

Confronting Miss Martin with the news was a pleasure she'd dreamed of for months.

"Really, I don't know what Miss Beecham will have to say about this," she commented sourly when Sally told her she was going back to the newsroom that day.

"If she has anything at all to say about it, she can say it to Mr. Hawker," Sally shrugged with unconcern, gathering up her belongings impatiently. Today no one, not even the thin-lipped Miss Martin, could ruin her joy. She felt as if an enormous black cloud had drifted from above her head, leaving the sun shining brightly through.

In the bustling city room she stood uncertainly for a moment, wondering where she should sit. One of the copyboys noticed her and came hurrying to relieve her of the arm of things she carried.

"Mr. McIntire said to clear your old desk for you," he informed her, leading the way. So she had been already expected, she realized happily.

She sat at her desk, looking around her as she had done on her first day on *The Globe*. The background din, the deafening clatter of typewriters, the constantly ringing telephones, and the impatient shouts for copyboys were all familiar, loved sounds. In a few moments, others in the room began to notice her and came over to welcome her back. Bill McIntire was busy behind the glass partition of his office but she saw him look up and give a welcoming nod in her direction. Her spirits soared.

As Sally hurried up the stairs of her apartment building one afternoon, Cathy popped out of her door and waved to her.

"Hi, Sal, I've got something for you," she called, ducking back into the door and emerging again with a prettily wrapped package. "Came by special delivery about an hour ago," she said, handing it over.

Puzzled, Sally took the small package from her. It was a white box, ornately bound with a profusion of scarlet ribbon. There was no indication as to who the sender was and she looked at Cathy with confusion.

The young nurse let out an envious wolf whistle. "That's some fancy-looking package there. Bet it's something terrifically expensive. Any idea who it's from?"

"None at all," Sally replied, looking at it with a frown.

"Well . . ." Cathy hinted with a comically eager look on her face.

"Oh, all right," Sally sighed with mock resignation. "I can see I'll be the subject of dreadful gossip and speculation in this house unless I let you see what it is right now."

"You can bet on it," Cathy assured her. "I've always wondered what such expensive-looking packages concealed, never having received one even remotely like it. Is it from Tiffany's? Cartier's? Come on, open up," she begged, rubbing her hands together with anticipation.

"Just to prove to you I have no secrets worth keeping," Sally laughed, and eased the ribbon off, then opened the lid. There, nestled between layers of tissue paper like a precious jewel, was a steel safety lock.

Cathy's jaw dropped in disappointment, but when she looked questioningly at Sally interest returned to her face, for Sally had turned bright pink.

"It's just a joke . . . a rather silly one," she muttered, fighting back a smile, and she dashed up the stairs leaving an even more curious Cathy behind her. Her heart was beating wildly as she opened her door with a key her hands were having trouble fitting into the lock. Once inside, she sat down in a chair with the box held gingerly in her lap, almost afraid to touch it.

Her fingers searched the box again but there was no card, no explanation. It would have been unnecessary; the message was very clear. She had not suspected Rafe Hawker capable of such a light-hearted gesture. His humor had always before held a measure of mockery and cynicism, but this was different. It was the recognition of a long-standing joke between them. Absently, she caressed her unglamorous gift as she sat deep in thought.

She realized that she must have been sitting like that for nearly an hour and, feeling rather foolish, she jumped to her feet. With recollection came a new, unnerving thought. She would have to thank him! No matter how lightheartedly it was meant, it also showed some concern for her safety and she couldn't altogether dismiss the gesture as a joke.

How should she thank him? To write a little note would be too formal and out of keeping with the spirit of the gift. She would have to thank him verbally and she would have to do it now. She was going home that evening to Glenbrook to spend Thanksgiving there and would not be back for a few days. It would be rude to leave it until then. The best thing would be to telephone, she decided. It was less personal and much easier than going to see him about it.

Sally reached for the phone quickly so as not to give herself time to get cold feet. She was nervous to a degree quite out of proportion with the nature of the gift and the motive behind it. By the time she completed dialing, she was praying fervently that he would be busy in a meeting or had already gone home.

She had to go through several people who all asked her name and business before she finally heard Eve Tarrant's now familiar voice.

"This is Mr. Hawker's secretary. Who's calling, please?"

"It's Sally Spencer, Mrs. Tarrant. Would it be possible to speak with Mr. Hawker?"

"Why, hello honey," the friendly voice replied, and she could almost hear the smile behind it. "I'm sure it is. Hold on a moment, will you? He's in some kind of conference but I'll see if he can talk to you."

"No, no . . . not if he's busy," Sally protested. "It's not very imp—" But Mrs. Tarrant had already cut her off to talk to her boss on the interoffice line. Fleetingly, Sally wondered why his secretary had taken such an obvious liking to her and how she had managed to earn the older woman's approval.

"Yes?" Hawker's abrupt voice cut into her thoughts.

Sally had to take a deep breath before she began. "It's Sally Spencer, Mr. Hawker. I did not mean to disturb you but I want to thank you for your . . . for the lock." This was not how she had meant to sound at all, she realized, with her breathless words echoing back to her. She had meant to sound as light as the gift had been. "It is very thoughtful of you."

"See to it that you have it installed at once. You'll need a professional locksmith," he advised.

"Yes, I'll get one as soon as I get back."

"Back? Back from where?" She thought the question was unnecessarily sharp.

"I'm going home for Thanksgiving today. I have a few days off."

There was a long pause and Sally wondered if he had put down the phone when his strong voice sounded again.

"I expect you will be seeing Mr. Smith then?" he queried.

"Yes, he knows I'm coming."

"Please give him my regards and tell him I'll be in touch very soon about those new presses we discussed. Oh, and Miss Spencer . . . try not to flood his office in tears this time or the old boy will think we are mistreating you here in New York." His insinuating laughter was the last thing Sally heard before she slammed the phone back in its cradle.

* * *

She chose to go home by train instead of flying, much to her Aunt Emily's relief, as she was a bundle of nerves every time one of her family traveled on a plane. The journey would take only a few hours and this way she would prolong the holiday mood and the anticipation of reaching home.

Sally was unashamedly sentimental about holidays and the frantic bustling scene at Penn Station increased her joy and excitement. She liked to imagine that all these people were jostling and hurrying for one purpose—to get to the various corners of the country for that special time tomorrow when everyone would be celebrating happily with family and friends.

She settled in a comfortable corner of her train and continued looking out her window even after it grew too dark to see anything but the warm lights of the many houses as she went rushing past. New York, *The Globe,* and everyone in it was already a world away. As long as she had her family and hometown to return to, nothing and no one else mattered so much.

When the train pulled into the quaint, familiar station a few hours later, she spotted her family on the platform at once—Aunt Emily holding the tiny mittened hand of a grandchild on each side, an anxious smile on her lips as she scanned the train windows in anticipation, Uncle John standing beside her with three of her cousins and an assortment of wildly romping dogs from various Holloway households.

When she stepped off the train, Sally was engulfed in one mass embrace as the family passed her around for kisses and hugs. The two small children tugged at her impatiently to be lifted and hugged, and the dogs, throwing themselves wholeheartedly into the homecoming, tried to outdo each other in shrill barking. Everything unpleasant that had happened to her since she was here last instantly faded away in the knowledge that she was to spend four blissful days with her family.

That night she slept a deep, carefree, and dreamless

sleep and woke to the noise of the household already stirring around her. Penny had already been let out, and after a long, luxurious stretch, Sally bounded out of bed and, pulling on a thick robe and warm slippers, raced for the bathroom. This was from an old habit, quite unnecessary these days as it had been a long time since the household's only overcrowded bathroom was the subject of many arguments among the younger Holloways.

The kitchen was bustling with activity and already emanating delicious smells when Sally went down for her breakfast. It was the sort of day that brought out the best in her aunt, with all the cooking and baking to do for the family meal that afternoon.

"Now I don't want you spending your day in the kitchen," her aunt scolded her, trying to take a flour sifter from her niece's hand. "The others are all out and about, and there's no need for you to stay cooped up in here with me."

"I certainly will," Sally insisted, taking the sifter back firmly. "You have no idea how much I've been looking forward to this. You wouldn't believe how tiny my kitchen is in New York; there's barely room enough to make an omelette, so I haven't had the chance to do any serious cooking. Besides, I'll have plenty of time to roam about in the next couple of days and I'd much rather spend today in this cozy kitchen with you."

Her aunt's protestations had been only half-hearted, as nothing gave her greater pleasure than to have her niece's help and company. It would give her a chance to talk to Sally alone.

The next few hours were spent filling pies, mixing sauces, roasting, basting, baking, while the two women chatted happily about family matters. Two large turkeys were turning golden in the oven in the full glory of Aunt Emily's special stuffing and basting sauce. Now that the Holloway family had swollen to include in-laws and grandchildren, one turkey was no longer enough; besides, Aunt Emily liked to have plenty left over to take to the elderly neighbors who couldn't cook a big meal for themselves.

Thanksgiving dinner was usually about three o'clock in the Holloway home, but long before this the family began drifting in and eventually ended up in the large kitchen where Aunt Emily kept shooing them from underfoot with good-natured tolerance.

When the Holloway children came to visit their parents, they brought with them their entire households, including dogs, cats, and, in the case of some of the more insistent grandchildren, even pet hamsters, rabbits, and tortoises. Through all the shouting, laughing, screaming, and barking, Emily and John Holloway remained serene and managed somehow to have the entire company freshly washed, brushed, and orderly at the table in time for grace.

The dinner lasted for more than three hours with long pauses between the courses. When the meal was at its height, with everyone fully engrossed in both the food and the conversation around the table, Sally felt herself drifting away from it all, her mind suddenly on Rafe Hawker.

Where was he having his Thanksgiving meal? she wondered. In some fancy restaurant, or being served by a butler in some rich household? Maybe even with Althea's family, she thought.

After the table had finally been cleared, Sally abandoned herself to her young cousins and spent the rest of the evening romping about with them, her full attention commanded by their games and adorable antics. Altogether it had been a perfect family day, she mused as she took a brisk walk before turning in that night. These late bedtime walks in fresh air were something she badly missed in Manhattan. They cleared the head so wonderfully and prepared one for sound, undisturbed sleep.

The next day, by standing arrangement, she called on Cornelius Smith. The old Patriot Building and ancient newspaper offices looked quaint compared to the impersonal vastness of the Globe Building. Her former colleagues welcomed her excitedly and it was a long while before an impatient Smithy could drag her away from their questioning and take her into his own office. For a moment after he closed the door, he held her hands in his and looked at her with affection.

"I'm glad to see you haven't changed at all since you left us," he observed, seating her in his own armchair. "You're not wearing any of that ghastly paint on your face and haven't dieted yourself away to one of those scarecrow figures that city girls like to affect these days. And that healthy bloom is still on your cheeks," he added with approval.

"What did you expect, a wasted, fallen woman to return from the city?" she laughed at him, coaxing a smile to his face. "It's only been four months, you know."

"Seems longer," he muttered. "I . . . that is, we, have missed you. You have done us very proud here. I've seen all your stories and I talked to Bill McIntire the other day. He's not an easy man to please, but he couldn't quite disguise his enthusiasm for you. Now tell me, dear, are *you* satisfied with the way everything is going?"

For the next hour they lapsed into newspaper talk and trade gossip. Despite his often disparaging remarks about New York and New York papers, Smithy looked at her with a hint of envy when she recounted some of the high points and near disasters she had experienced on *The Globe.*

"Not much of that sort of thing happens around here," he conceded, adding defensively, "but mind you, we get our fair share of excitement."

They chatted for a while longer. Then, as Sally was saying good-bye to him, she sudenly remembered. "By the way, Rafe Haw— Mr. Hawker asked me to give you a message. He sends his regards and says he'll be in touch with you soon about some presses you had discussed." She managed to sound nonchalant but pronouncing his name in this very room brought back some unpleasant memories. His last admonishment, "Try not to flood his office in tears . . ." echoed in her ears.

"Good, very good," said Smithy with satisfaction. "See much of him, by the way?"

"No, not really," she answered vaguely. "Nobody does."

"Just wondered how he came to give you the message, that's all," he said with a sly look at her.

Sally chose to ignore this and planting a kiss on his cheek, left him to make her round of visits in town.

Sally's last day at home was spent in saying farewells to the people she had been greeting just three days before. From the downcast way her aunt packed her case, Sally knew that she was acutely disappointed. It seemed that she had hoped that once her niece was back in the family fold, she would find it impossible to go away again.

Sally's spirits, too, were at a low. It wasn't that she did not love her job; in fact, she was eager to get back to it. But New York also meant the end of her peace of mind and the beginning of inevitable problems. Although her life had become relatively uncomplicated since she had parted company with Althea, some apprehension still clung to her.

An hour before her New York–bound train was due, she stood in the living room surrounded by the family. Aunt Emily busied herself to hide her distress but the others were talking and laughing with animation. In the general confusion no one heard the bell ring at first. It was one of the dogs that alerted them to the fact that there was someone at the door.

"I'll get it," Sally volunteered and, collaring the barking dogs, cleared a space to open the front door.

"I'm afraid you'll have to step over these brutes . . ." she began, but her laughter died when she looked up.

"Noisy bunch, aren't they?" Rafe Hawker remarked,

his eyes taking in her glowing cheeks, still flushed from the warmth of the fire in the living room, and her slightly tousled hair, a result of struggling with the dogs. The next moment his attention was claimed by the animals, which tried to jump up at him in friendly greeting. "That's enough now, fellows," he told them in a low, firm voice, and magically the dops stopped their welcoming assaults on him and subsided into tail wagging and sniffing at the visitor.

Sally was in a state of paralysis, quite unable to move, staring at him with unbelieving eyes.

"At least the dogs know how to make a visitor feel welcome, even if you don't," he commented, patting them on the head.

She recovered herself just enough to open the door wider but her voice came out in a high-pitched squeak when she stammered, "I'm sorry. . . . It's just that . . . you are probably the last person I expected to see here." Recovering herself a little more, she asked abruptly, "Come to think of it, what *are* you doing here?"

"That's what I call a really gracious hostess," he remarked to the dogs conversationally. "Does she always keep her guests standing on the doorstep while giving them the third degree?"

Sally blurted out an apology and invited him into the living room to meet her family. When she walked in with him and introduced him, the others had the polite good sense to hide their surprise and greeted him as if he were an ordinary, welcome visitor. Only Aunt Emily was making huge, questioning eyes at Sally, but she was too nonplussed herself to do more than give a faint shrug in answer.

To her astonishment, Hawker was drawn into conversation by her uncle and cousins at once and she thought she had never seen him quite so much at ease. He talked freely with them of trivial matters that she would have believed quite beneath the aloof, arrogant publisher of *The Globe*. Sally herself contributed little to the conversation, her mind too intent on working out the reason for his being here in her house. She sat perched on the arm of her uncle's chair and looked at him out of the corner of her eye.

He was dressed more casually than she had seen him before, a thick wool sweater with a tweed jacket to match his slacks; without his usual formal air he appeared to be younger looking. He leaned back, completely relaxed in his chair, ignoring Sally and focusing all his attention on what her uncle was telling him.

Why was he here? The thought hammered insistently in her mind. Am I dreaming this, or is that really Rafe Hawker sitting here chatting with my family as if it were the most natural thing for him to drop in for a visit? Even if he decided to come to see Smithy, what would make him come *here*? Why wouldn't he have gone to *The Patriot* and then right back to New York?

New York! "My God!" The exclamation escaped her. "My train, it will be here any minute. I'll miss it."

"There's plenty of time," Hawker cut in with a brief glance in her direction. "I'm driving back to New York. I'll take you back in my car."

As usual, it was not so much an invitation as a statement of fact, but instead of provoking her annoyance, this time it aroused quite a different feeling.

"I had some business with Cornelius Smith at *The Patriot* so I drove down earlier today." His explanation was directed at Uncle John but she knew it was meant for her.

Immediately, Aunt Emily's instincts as a hostess were aroused. "In that case, after all that driving, you could probably do with a hot meal. I hopee you will stay for dinner with us. I can fix up something in no time at all."

"I'd like nothing better," he smiled at her.

Aunt Emily nodded with satisfaction and made her way to the kitchen with Sally following close at her heels.

"I think you should go back inside. It's not polite to leave your guest, dear," she scolded her niece. "Unless, of course, there is something you want to tell me," she hinted slyly.

"Tell you?" Sally repeated with pretended indifference. "Why, I couldn't be more surprised myself. I'm as astonished at his being here as you are."

"I'm not in the least astonished," her aunt denied. "Who says I'm astonished? The only thing that surprises me," she added with a mischievous smile, "is that he's nothing like the person some people like to hint he is. I think he is friendly and polite—and handsome too."

"Handsome?" Sally wondered.

"Don't you think so, dear?" Aunt Emily asked, and smiled knowingly when she saw her niece blush. Thinking the matter over, she added, "I imagine an attractive man like him would be very popular with women. Is he courting anyone, do you know?"

"No, I don't know," Sally shrugged, smiling at her aunt's old-fashioned word. "I rather think they court him. At least I've heard he has plenty of women friends." She hoped she sounded indifferent enough to convince her aunt.

"And you, darling? How well do you know him?" Emily Holloway asked casually.

"Not well." Sally was flustered now. "Hardly at all." Catching her aunt's speculative look, she exclaimed with exasperation, "Oh, aunt, really. You're way off the track in your matchmaking this time. Why, Rafe Hawker is the very last man . . . if you only knew . . ." She broke off in total confusion, blushing violently.

"All I do know is that the man happened to drive all the way down here at the same time you just happened to be home on a visit, and he is sitting in our living room right now, waiting to drive you back to New York," Aunt Emily insisted stubbornly.

It would be futile to try to convince her devoted aunt that Rafe Hawker was just not the sort of man you started romantic speculations about, that he was too haughty, too rich, and too powerful, and that he treated her alternately with condescending amusement or contemptuous sarcasm, and was only seen in the company of pedigreed women like Althea Beecham. That would not be the way her aunt would see it at all. To her, the most natural thing in the world was for a man, no matter how mighty and powerful, to be bewitched by her golden-haired, sweet-natured, spirited, and clever niece.

"And now, dear," her aunt concluded in firm tones, "kindly get out of my kitchen and get back into the living room at once or your visitor will think that I did not teach my family very good manners."

Sally returned to the living room where the others were deep in discussion. The Holloway family was naturally extroverted and Hawker appeared to fit right in. He lounged in his chair, engrossed in conversation, while one of the dogs that had rested his head on his knee was enjoying the firm caresses of those long, strong fingers. Hawker looked up and gave Sally a passing glance as she came back into the room; then his attention went back to one of her cousins, who at that moment was talking to him.

From a shadowy corner Sally looked on, a wild happiness she had never experienced before surging through her at the scene. Seeing Hawker like this, stretched out before a glowing fire, surrounded by her family who all seemed to take a liking to him, filled her with a melting warmth. She no longer cared why he was here, all she knew was that for the moment he belonged in this room as no outsider ever had.

She paid little heed to the conversation. Instead, her eyes were busy searching his face, so open now, so ready to break into a smile or a laugh. The ice had melted from his gray eyes and there were soft lines where she had seen only grimness before. In a dream-like trance her eyes lingered on the hands slowly strok-

ing the dog's head and she remembered with a little
shiver that she knew what those hands felt like.

Her daydreaming was interrupted by Aunt Emily's
announcement that dinner was waiting on the dining-
room table. Hawker excused himself to wash up, and
looking out the window, Sally noticed with surprise
that the late afternoon had already turned into velvet,
dark evening.

Over dinner, the easy, relaxed mood continued and
Sally, who had been seated next to Hawker on her
aunt's quiet insistence, forgot her self-consciousness
enough to join in, though she was too excited and apprehensive to do more than pick at her food. The visitor, on the other hand, ate heartily and went up even
higher in Emily Holloway's estimation by praising her
cooking handsomely.

"It's a shame you couldn't have been here for
Thanksgiving dinner, then," Uncle John spoke up.
"Emily really outdid herself for that."

"I regret it too," Hawker replied with a side glance
at Sally. "Of course, if I had been invited, I would
have gratefully accepted." This last had been directed
at Sally in a low voice but it caught her aunt's ear.

"There, you see?" she turned to her niece reproach-
fully.

"I thought you probably regarded Thanksgiving as
foolish, sentimental nonsense," Sally said defensively.

"I do have some measure of sentiment in me, despite
your opinion to the contrary, you know," he murmured.

Sally lowered her eyes to her plate and said nothing.

"Mom's Thanksgiving dinner is nothing compared
to the feast she cooks up for Christmas," her cousin
Joanne threw in. She winked at Sally. "Maybe you
could come and eat with us then."

Sally felt all eyes on her at that moment and she
was too busy trying to keep her composure to hear
Hawker's reply.

It was a new experience to watch Rafe Hawker

make a deliberate attempt to be charming. She had never before seen him trouble himself about putting people at ease, yet that was exactly what he was doing now.

All too soon it was time to break up the party and start for New York. Aunt Emily pressed a thermos of hot coffee and a package of sandwiches on her niece for the long journey ahead, as she gave her a last hug at the door, and Hawker shook hands all around.

As he helped her into his car the comfortable, warm feeling that had enveloped her all evening vanished, nervousness taking its place. She was alone with him now and would be for the next few hours. Would his easy mood continue or would he lapse into one of his impenetrable silences?

They drove off into the darkness with a final wave at the family assembled on the porch. The car was not the limousine she had seen him use around town but a smaller model, ideal for the rough country roads. In no time at all a comfortable warmth flooded its interior and she unbuttoned the heavy coat she had put on for the journey.

"Is it too hot for you?" he asked. "I can turn the heater down if you'd like."

"No, it's just fine," she murmured, settling back against her seat. She stole a look at him and saw that he was perfectly at ease, his hands holding the wheel lightly but with assurance, his eyes slightly narrowed, scanning the dark road ahead. He turned his head abruptly and caught her stare.

"You're not nervous, by any chance?" he suggested with raised eyebrows.

"Not in the least," Sally replied and, deliberately misunderstanding, added, "I'm quite used to night driving."

Hawker laughed softly, knowing that she had understood his real meaning. "So you don't mind driving to New York, then, instead of catching the train?"

"No, it's really very kind of you," she replied politely and added with unexpected boldness, "though I was a little surprised at you turning up in Glenbrook like this. Why did you?"

For a moment he didn't reply, and she thought with a feeling of immediate regret that she had gone too far. Then, as if having given it some consideration, he replied, "I told you. I came to see Smithy on business."

"Coincidence, isn't it?" The daring words were out of her mouth before she had time to check them.

"It is rather," he turned to her with a wide grin. "Unless, of course, you interpret it that I came down here deliberately to see you."

Not knowing what to say, she turned her head away and looked out the window. Hawker reached a hand out and, taking her by the chin, turned her face toward him.

Sally started at the unexpected contact and let out an audible gasp.

His face took on a look of astonishment and he pulled the car over to the shoulder of the road. This time he reached out deliberately to turn her face toward him.

Unsure of herself, she forced an unsteady smile on her face. "I'm sorry, I didn't mean to react like that. I'm a little jumpy, I guess," she murmured in apology.

"Why are you jumpy?" he asked her.

Because I'm a fool, Sally thought. Because just sitting in the same car with you completely destroys my composure, and being so close to you seems to be more than I can handle. But she remained silent, keeping her eyes downcast.

"You had better make up your mind whether you want to be provocative with me or demure," he advised, adding in a voice almost too low to hear, "I don't care which it is. I like you either way."

Sliding one hand behind her head to the back of her neck, he held her chin with the other and moved closer. His kiss was slow and steady, his lips firm and hot on her own. Sally felt the blood drain out of her, leaving her body limp. She felt herself sink helplessly and clutched tentatively at the front of his jacket with both hands. Hawker drew back for a moment and looked down at her intensely. There was no mockery in his eyes, only a steady, wondering look.

Sally felt utterly drained, the power of his kiss still coursing through her. To escape his unwavering gaze, she bowed her head and leaned her forehead weakly against his chest. Hawker stroked her hair for a moment, then tilting her face up gently, he held his lips against her temple.

An urgency rose in her and, drawing her arms about his neck, she offered him her lips again. He took them, this time with more force, more demand, and she met pressure for breathless pressure, leaning against the back of the seat, pulling his body with her. His lips locked on hers for a long moment, his body pressing the breath out of her, then almost abruptly he wrenched himself away.

"Sweet, sweet Sally," he murmured into her hair, his voice low and thick. For an instant an almost insane happiness seized her. If she could only stay like this forever, with her head over his heart, breathing in his faint, pleasantly masculine smell, and never have to look up again to see what the expression in his eyes might be. She gave a long shuddering sigh and pulled away.

By the time she did dare to glance at him, Hawker was sitting back against his side of the seat, his glance on her direct but wary. Her wide eyes and tousled hair made her look very young and vulnerable.

"You're very lovely," he murmured, almost to himself. Recollection seemed to come to him then and he drew himself straighter. "We had better get going," he said quietly, starting the car.

Sally plunged from the joy of a moment before into the depths of despair. Please, she prayed silently, please don't let him regret what just happened. Please let it mean to him what it meant to me. Her eyes searched his face for some explanation of his sudden change of mood. Had she been wrong to return his kiss so hungrily? Had it been wrong to show how much she wanted it? All she knew was that she would have given her life to him had he asked for it during those moments in his arms.

This time Hawker did make an attempt to ease the tension and gradually conversation started up between them, as his skilled driving swallowed up the miles. He did most of the talking while Sally did her best to make her response cheerful, fighting down the pain that was tearing at her heart. His tone was softer than usual, without the customary sarcastic edge to it, but he gave no other hint of what had just passed between them. She remembered sadly how, on that occasion in her apartment when he had first showed her his gentle side, he had reacted with the same abrupt change of mood. There was a definite shield around him, she realized, and the fact that it had been lowered for a short time tonight made it all the harder for her to bear to see it firmly back in place again.

Hawker mistook her silence for tiredness and offered, "If you are getting tired, don't hesitate to curl up and get some sleep."

"I'm not sleepy, I'm wide awake," she assured him, fighting to keep the numbness out of her voice.

"Good. I'd much rather you kept me company." She looked at his shadowed profile, thinking that even those lightly said words were a balm to the ache inside her.

Then she remembered her aunt's package and offered, "It would probably do you good to rest for a while and have some coffee. Aunt Emily has packed us a thermos and some sandwiches."

"Blessed Aunt Emily," he smiled, pulling up by the side of the road for the second time that night. A little shiver ran through Sally as the car stopped, but she busied herself with pouring out the strong, steaming coffee and unwrapping the sandwiches. Hawker accepted the hot drink but declined the sandwich.

"It's going to get cold now that I've turned the motor

off. You'd better move closer to me to keep warm."
The suggestion was made lightly, almost impersonally.

Sally hesitated but he drew her toward him, prop-
ping her lightly against his lean, hard body. With one
arm he encircled her shoulders loosely, the other held
his steaming mug. It was the sort of protective
gesture one would make toward a child, but instantly
the warm feeling of contentment surged through Sally
anew. Turned as she was with her back slightly to him,
she could not see his face and she was glad he could
not see her own, so openly full of longing. Her heart-
beats thundered in her ears and she wondered in alarm
if he could hear them.

Outside, there was a dark, chill stillness which inten-
sified their closeness in the car, giving her the feeling
that the two of them were alone in the world. She
shivered with the intensity of her longing.

"Cold?" he asked, and pulled his arm a little tighter
around her. Sally surrendered herself to the moment
and, leaning against him, closed her eyes. Come what
may, she would savor every second of these few precious minutes sitting in the shelter of his arms. No
matter what happened in the future, this moment
could never be taken from her.

She stirred only to pour him a second cup, then his
arm was back around her again and she accepted its
protection willingly. Her mind was void of everything
except the vivid awareness of him as they sat in silence.

Finally Hawker stirred and gently put her from him,
saying, "We should be on our way."

Once the car was back on the road, Hawker seemed
deeply preoccupied, and this time it was Sally who
made the effort to keep a light conversation going. To
sit there in silence would have plunged her too painfully into thoughts which she preferred to keep at bay
right now. For the rest of the journey she was determined to make herself seem lighthearted. She would
die before she let him glimpse the depths of her feelings. The closer they came to the city, the more remote

she imagined he was getting, as if they were speeding back toward reality from the temporary lapse he had allowed himself back there on the dark country road.

When she finally saw the pinpoint lights of Manhattan in the distance, her heart sank heavily and an ache clutched her throat. The night was ending and there would never be another like it again, she told herself, the thought giving her a sickeningly empty feeling.

Sooner, much sooner than she would have thought possible, they were pulling up outside her apartment. After he turned off the motor, he did not make a move but sat motionless, looking out into the night with a faraway look.

Sally's heart began thundering inside her; she was again aware of a state of suspension, waiting for the outcome of the struggle that seemed to be going on inside him. She held her breath and willed him to say whatever it was he had already twice been on the verge of telling her.

Hawker felt her gaze on him and turned to her. At once he was back on his guard, composed, having apparently won the struggle with himself once more. Whatever the emotion had been, he had fought it and managed to suppress it. It would never win, never be allowed to surface, she told herself in despair.

Forcing a tremulous smile of her own, she blurted out a hasty thanks for the drive home. The memory of the evening and her own pent-up longings mocked her, making her words sound trite and artificial.

It was a matter of urgency now to get away from him, to be alone with her thoughts.

He caught the tremor in her voice and looked at her tenderly. Tearing her eyes away, she offered a hasty explanation. "I guess I'm much more tired than I thought. Now that we're home, I can't keep my eyes open." She blinked as if to prove it, but it was the prickling of tears, not tiredness, that made her eyes heavy.

With one curious, searching look, he got out of the

car and held her door open. They walked to the front entrance and she turned to him wearily. "I'll say good night to you here. You must be exhausted from all that driving and anxious to get home."

"I'll walk you upstairs to your door, just to make sure you are safe," he said firmly, and obediently she allowed him to lead her up the stairs.

He took the keys from her hand, pushed the door open and, after turning on the light switch by the door, glanced briefly around but did not step inside.

"All safe," he told her with a smile. "Which reminds me," he added. "Promise me you'll have that lock fitted to your door tomorrow."

I'll promise you anything you ask me, she silently vowed, but aloud said, "I promise."

Again he hesitated as he looked down at her, but the next moment he brushed her cheek lightly with his hand and, turning, bounded down the stairs.

Sally closed the door behind her and, leaning against it, let the ache wash through her with full force.

"God help me," she whispered into the lonely silence. "How did I fall in love with Rafe Hawker?"

CHAPTER NINE

In the days ahead Sally went through the motions of working, doing her chores at home, and going out with friends with all the emotional involvement of a robot. The pain she felt on the night when Hawker brought her home and she admitted to herself for the first time that she was in love with him had gradually subsided into a weary melancholy, the shattering realization firmly tucked away somewhere in the recesses of her mind. She wasn't sure which was worse, the pain she had first felt or the aching void that had taken its place. Since that night he hadn't made even the smallest attempt to see her.

She had realized that night that she had been in love with Hawker for a long time, perhaps even as far back as their first meeting in Glenbrook when one glance from him had been enough to make her heart beat wildly. Even then he had aroused in her an emotion she'd never felt before. But she was certain love had really taken hold on the night when he had first come to her apartment. One unexpectedly tender gesture from him had been enough to capture her heart.

Stupid, foolish creature, she reproved herself time and time again. Of all the men in the world, how could she have fallen in love with Rafe Hawker? Even worse, how could she have allowed him to *see* that she had fallen in love with him? She had made it so very clear on the drive back from Glenbrook.

He probably felt sorry for her, she agonized, after he witnessed how his kisses had worked on her; that was why he had been so thoughtfully quiet during the rest of the drive home.

And yet, the argument arose in her mind, it had never been she who had sought him out; if anything, she had done her best to keep out of his way. It hadn't been she who intruded on him that night in the Chantilly Room, nor the one who had gone looking for him at The Headliner on a flimsy pretext. She had not been the one who had arranged a business trip to Glenbrook to coincide with his own visit there. What had he wanted from her on those occasions? her heart demanded, while her mind was trying to impose logic on her emotions.

There was also the one irrevocable fact that nothing could explain away: There was Althea.

Sally had not seen Hawker since their return from

Glenbrook more than a week before, but she had heard through the grapevine that he had gone away somewhere on vacation. When she noticed that Althea's social columns were being written from a luxurious ski resort in Colorado, it was not hard to put two and two together.

A visit to her desk from Mike Costello left her in no doubt.

After some cursory chatter, he launched right in. "A friend of mine has just returned from a ski lodge near Aspen," he dropped a shade too casually.

Cold fingers were clutching at her stomach and she realized what was coming but managed to keep a look of polite interest on her face.

"You'd never guess what twosome he spotted there," he pursued, the spite in his voice unmistakable.

"No, I probably never would, so I won't waste my time trying," Sally agreed with forced composure.

"None other than the Hawk himself in the cozy company of Althea Beecham." He watched her closely for the effect of this information, but Sally managed an indifferent shrug.

"So?"

Mike, whose voice had been full of satisfaction, looked disappointed now. He looked at her sharply but her returning glance revealed nothing.

"You're either a very cool young lady, or very sure of yourself," he debated aloud. When Sally did not respond, he changed his manner, as if suddenly hit by a fresh idea.

"It's been ages since we've had a chance to talk, Sal. How about having dinner with me? How about tonight?"

Sally had never realized before just how much dislike she had stored up for Mike Costello. She wondered with an inward shudder how she could ever have thought him charming or good company, how she could ever have endured his conceit and impertinence. People like Mike, who flourished on nothing but ego, harbored grudges forever against people who had damaged their vanity. They did not have the character to fight out in the open, so instead they sought revenge in secret ways. Sally realized with chilling certainty that Mike no longer really liked her, that he was still persisting in his attentions only to salve the ego she had helped to wound. Alienated, he could be a dangerous enemy.

"No, Mike, I don't think so, thank you. I'm pretty busy these days." She did not enjoy rejecting people, not even someone like Mike, and hoped that he would understand her refusal for what it was, without forcing her to put it into stronger words for him.

It was clear from his hardened expression that he understood, but he was not prepared to retreat in dignity as she had hoped he would.

"Still holding out for the big one, Sal?" he asked viciously. "You're wasting your time, you know. No dame ever stays a permanent fixture with Hawker and I've seen him have his choice of the best of them. Maybe you would like me around to pick up the pieces when you finally realize that." Angrily, he stalked away.

The words echoed in Sally's ears a long time after Mike had left. They had been said in fury but she recognized some truth in them. "I've seen him have his choice of the best of them." Yes, a multitude of choices, she considered bitterly, but Mike had been wrong when he said none of them stayed a permanent fixture. Every indication pointed to the fact that Althea had changed that and had become permanent in his life. Sally struggled in vain against the despair that overwhelmed her.

In the following days she threw herself into her work with an exhausting intensity, deliberately tiring herself out so by the time she reached home at night she was too numb with weariness to feel anything else.

One afternoon she was returning from an interview with Sam Allen, the young photographer with whom she had shared several assignments before. Sam had taken his own car with him to the interview and they were driving through the West Side on their way back to the office.

Sally was absorbed in the majestic old apartment houses of the once elegant and exclusive area overlooking the Hudson River. This was her favorite part of town and she turned to Sam.

"One day when I have the money, I'm going to move into one of these apartment houses right here. Some of them are quite palatial looking from the outside and I bet the insides match. I went on a story to one of them a couple weeks ago and it was the most beautiful apartment I had ever seen. Had about ten rooms, all with huge fireplaces."

"I like these old town houses in the side streets myself," Sam said.

"Oh, yes, but you'd have to be a millionaire to live in one of those," she sighed.

"Want to see a really beautiful one? You'll be surprised at who it belongs to," he offered eagerly, a mischievous look in his eyes.

"Okay," Sally agreed, and in a few minutes Sam was stopping the car on a quiet, tree-lined street with beautifully kept town houses.

"Guess who lives in that one?" he grinned, pointing to a house opposite.

Sally surveyed the tall, narrow building, its ancient face covered in ivy vines, its brass fixtures winking brightly in the afternoon sun. There was a massive wrought iron and glass front door and Sally caught the gleam of a dazzling chandelier through its clear glass fanlight. Puzzled, she turned at Sam.

"Some swell joint, eh? Aren't you going to take a guess?" the young man asked triumphantly.

"I know, don't tell me," Sally teased. "It belongs to you. I always suspected you photographers were overpaid."

Sam's grin widened but before he could reply a

beautifully groomed red setter spotted the open window of the car and raced over to them, doing his best to climb inside.

Laughingly Sally patted the sleek silken head and with renewed enthusiasm the dog tried to wriggle in through the window. Sally's laughter was cut short by the sound of a commanding voice.

"Get down, you silly devil! You can't invade people's cars like that!"

Even before the figure made its appearance at the window Sally felt a shock jolt through her. In the next second, the long frame was stooping down, the words of apology arrested on his lips at the sight of her. Steel gray eyebrows shot up and the firm mouth curled with amusement.

Blanching, Sally stared helplessly into Rafe Hawker's unwavering granite eyes. It was then humiliatingly obvious that it was his house she had been staring at.

"Why, Miss Spencer, what an unexpected surprise," he said with irony, straightening up to his full height. He was wearing a turtleneck pullover under his sheepskin jacket, seemingly out for a walk with his dog.

Sally shot an accusing glance at Sam, who had slipped into a state of shock at the unexpected apparition of *The Globe*'s publisher. Nervously, he cleared his throat and stammered, "It's all my fault, sir, I'm sorry. I brought Sally here. . . . She didn't know . . ." His voice trailed away uncertainly under the publisher's amused glance.

"Are you two keeping my house under surveillance by any chance?" Hawker asked with fascination.

"No . . . it's nothing like that, sir," Sam protested. "I just . . ." The young man gulped, but Hawker's attention was already back on Sally.

She sat with her eyes closed, fists clenched in her lap. This can't be happening, her brain screamed in protest. How must this look to him, what must he be thinking of her? "Are *you* keeping my house under

surveillance?" The sarcastic words burned into her.
Oh, damn, that's exactly how it must look to him. If
only Sam had warned me, I could have stopped him.
This is the most humiliating thing that has ever happened. Somehow she must make Hawker see that she
wasn't here to spy on him. With resolve she opened
her eyes and braced herself.

Before she had a chance to speak, Hawker deliberately cut her off. "Since you *have* come all this way to
call on me, do come inside, Miss Spencer."

"I did not come to call on you," Sally began through
clenched teeth, but he ignored her and turned to Sam.

"And you, I'm sure, have some important things to
do back in the office, young man." His tone did not invite argument. Sam, torn between sticking by Sally
and the relief that he was being dismissed, hesitated,
but Hawker had already opened Sally's door and was
pointedly waiting for her to get out. He always managed to put her in a position where it was wiser to
acquiesce than to argue with him. Feeling like the
proverbial lamb led to slaughter, she got out of the
car.

She darted a fleeting glance at Sam that started out
to be accusing but changed to a reassuring smile when
she saw the stricken look on his face. Even in her own
predicament, she had time to feel a little sorry for him.
Relieved by her smile, he started up the car none too
carefully and, making an awkward and illegal U turn,
disappeared around the corner. Sally looked after him
with considerable envy.

Now she was alone with Hawker and decided to face
him squarely. "I did not come here deliberately and
we were most certainly not spying on you," she said in
answer to the amused gleam in his eyes.

"Let's not discuss that here, all right?" he said dryly,
and taking her by the elbow, he steered her toward
the house. "This way," he instructed. The dog bounded
happily ahead of them up the short flight of steps to
the front entrance.

For a second Sally hesitated, looking up at the building with apprehension. She had an insane notion that there was danger for her inside that house. If she went in, she would be that much more involved with him; if she had a glimpse of his private world, it would mean another memory she would have to struggle to forget.

Hawker noted her reluctance and took a firmer grip on her elbow. "Please don't look at my house as if it were a notorious den of sin. You'll be perfectly safe, I can assure you. Every young lady who has ever ventured inside was able to leave it completely unharmed."

Sally allowed herself to be led to the front door, which Hawker opened and held wide for her. Despite her trepidation and embarrassment, she stopped short after the first few steps and looked about her with undisguised admiration.

The house's narrow exterior belied the spaciousness of its interior. The wide hall in which they were standing was high ceilinged, wonderfully spacious. Its floor of black-and-white marble squares was partly covered by an emerald green rug. Two large mirrors with gold leaf frames reflected the soft light of the crystal chandelier, and potted palms stood in large brass containers along the walls. The only furniture in the hall was a rococo marble and ormolu hall table.

At the far end Sally could see a spiral staircase leading to the upper floors. The entrance hall had an aura of splendor without being ostentatious, the same curious effect of spartan luxury as his office.

Hawker took her coat from her. "Let's go in here." He indicated a door to the left. They entered what she judged to be a living room or salon, and at a glance she saw it was furnished with some excellent pieces of antique furniture yet had an air of inviting comfort about it. The furnishings were a mixture of Regency and the less ornate styles of French Empire. Oriental rugs covered most of the dark polished floor, and a large collection of oils and watercolors, mostly land-

scapes, lined the walls. A fire was blazing in a large
fireplace which was built at an angle in one corner.

The various pieces in the room had obviously been
chosen with discrimination, by Hawker himself instead of an interior decorator, Sally was certain, yet
the room stopped just short of being personal. There
was the same absence of photographs or personal
mementos that had struck her in his office.

Sally had been so lost in admiring her surroundings
that she realized with embarrassment that while she
had been appraising the room, Hawker had been appraising her.

"Do you approve?" he asked.

"I'm sure everyone who sees it does," Sally replied,
determined to sound casual.

"But everyone doesn't matter."

Sally's heart gave a wild lurch. He had the power to
do that to her every time he carelessly threw one of
his ambiguous lines her way. Careful, she warned herself quickly. Don't let your imagination run away with
you again.

"Come sit down by the fire," Hawker invited, and
she followed him obediently. She chose an armchair
instead of the velvet settee that could seat both of
them. The red setter immediately stretched himself out
near the fire by her feet.

"What's his name?" Sally asked, stroking his silken
fur.

"I call him all sorts of uncomplimentary names because he is a hopelessly silly dog and nothing much
can be done with him. But in polite company he is
called Tom." At the sound of his name the setter
leaped up awkwardly, knocking over a small side
table, and made loving assaults on his master, his wagging tail creating a whirlwind.

"See what I mean?" Hawker asked, warding off the
dog and forcing him to lie down again. Sally was surprised at his patience and affection for the clumsy, ill-
trained animal. She would have imagined him to be

a much sterner master, someone who kept his dog at heel as he did his people.

"Let's have something to drink," Hawker suggested, "and then I'll take you out to dinner."

"Dinner?" Sally repeated, startled.

"Yes, surely you've heard of the idea before. And don't make it sound as if it was a dishonorable proposition. You don't have other plans for the evening, do you?" he asked casually.

Sally shook her head, happiness flowing through her, all resolutions to keep on her guard melting away.

"Good, now what would you like to drink?"

"Some white wine, please?"

While he was gone to fix the drinks, Sally fought a familiar struggle with herself and lost. She knew she would have to pay the price for whatever pleasure tonight offered, but she was too excited to feel more than a distant apprehension.

Recklessly, she would surrender for one last time to him, allow herself to look at his face, listen to his voice, and hope for one of his rare smiles. She trusted him; it was her own emotions she feared, but they could be dealt with tomorrow and in the long empty days ahead.

Hawker returned with a bottle of chilled wine on a tray, then poured himself a drink from a decanter on the rosewood sideboard and brought her a crystal wine glass. When he poured the wine, her eyes met his and she ventured a tentative smile. He returned it and kept his gaze on her face. As always, this had the effect of making her heart race dizzyingly, pumping color to her cheeks. She lowered her eyes and sipped her drink.

Feeling that she had nothing to lose, she decided to ask him some questions, something she had always avoided doing before.

"Have you lived in this house for long?" she asked, looking about her.

"I bought it ten years ago," he replied, apparently

not minding her inquisitiveness, "but I didn't live here for the first few years. I moved around too much to settle in one place." That would have been during the years when he was buying up papers all over the country, she calculated.

"And are you settled in New York for good now?" she asked.

"That is my intention," he replied. "Are you?"

"Staying in New York for good? Oh, for the time being anyway, as long as my job lasts, and I hope that will be a good while."

"Is that what you want out of life? A good job?" he asked seriously. It was amazing how quickly he could deflect questions away from himself and skillfully turn them to satisfy his own curiosity.

"Right now it is," she replied with conviction.

"I wonder where you get your ambitious streak. None of the others in your family struck me that way," he mused, looking at her through narrowed eyes.

"You sound as if you don't approve of the fact that I love my job and mean to be dedicated to it," she said a little defensively.

"Generally I admire dedication, especially when it is displayed by my own employees," he drawled, "but in your case . . . you're right, I don't altogether approve."

His direct gaze disconcerted her and the question died on her lips. She was too afraid of the answer he might give if she asked his meaning, afraid it would destroy the composure she had been making an effort to keep. The conversation was getting personal again, and nervously, she tried to divert it with the first thing that came to her mind.

"It must have taken you a very long time to collect all this." She gestured with her arm around the room.

Hawker smiled at her transparency but replied to her question. "Not very long; I wouldn't have had the time for that. I picked up most of these things at one or two auctions in Europe." Sally hoped he would continue on the subject, but he didn't volunteer any more details.

She had never known anyone who talked less about himself than Hawker. She supposed she knew him better by now than most others on *The Globe,* yet she knew not much more about his background now than she had before they met. In all their conversations he had always been the one to ask the questions, she the one to give the answers. She did not believe he deliberately went out of his way to be mysterious, nor did she think he had dark secrets to hide. He simply had a very real aversion to revealing anything of himself, to giving anything away. Hawker was probably the most completely withdrawn person she had ever known. That was why those fleeting, infrequent moments when he let down his guard left a more lasting impression on her than anything had ever done.

She accepted another glass of wine and allowed herself to relax with its soothing effect. She felt the same mellowness she had experienced when he had been one of her family circle for that brief evening at Thanksgiving. Carelessly she wondered how her heart could so easily be lulled into such happiness, when she well knew its cause was only momentary, and that when she went home it would be over, replaced by the familiar aching despair.

For the first time it occurred to Sally that she had not really explained, at least not to her own satisfaction, how she had happened to be outside his house. She couldn't let him go on thinking it was deliberate; she could not allow herself to look that much of a fool in his eyes.

"I didn't have the chance to explain . . . about being here in the first place," she began haltingly. "It really was quite unintentional. I hope you—"

"That was quite obvious from the ghostly pallor your face took on when you saw me," he cut in with a laugh. "Must you look at me with quite that much aversion every time we meet, by the way?"

"It's just that it always happens under such awkward circumstances," she demurred.

"Did you find my coming to Glenbrook such an awkward circumstance?"

"No," she allowed, adding to herself that it was the most wonderful thing that had ever happened to her.

"Yet it took you half the night to get over what seemed like an unpleasant shock."

"It was not in the least unpleasant," she protested quickly. "It was just a . . . surprise."

"Have you wondered why I just happened to be in your hometown at that particular time?"

"You told me that you came there on business, to see Smithy," Sally replied, trying to sound offhand, but the question she had asked in the car on their drive back and what it had led to was still fresh in her memory. Trying to hide her embarrassment, she leaned forward and patted the dog. Her hair swung forward to form a protective veil around her face.

"And you believed that?" he asked, with a laugh that sent shivers over her body.

"Of course," she murmured.

Hawker took her by the shoulders and made her sit up to face him. "Then you are the most artless woman I have ever met," he said softly, brushing her hair back. "The reason I went to Glenbrook at that particular time—as it must have been plainly obvious to everyone but you—was to see you, of course, and to have the pleasure of driving back to New York with you. Oh, and also to meet your Aunt Emily."

"Aunt Emily?" she repeated, wide eyed. "Why?"

Hawker looked at her disturbingly for a moment, then laughed. "If I told you it was because I found you the most fascinating woman I have ever met, would you believe it?"

Sally shook her head, her brows drawing together. Was he making fun of her?

"I thought that sort of flattering nonsense would not hold water with you," he nodded. "Very well then. I went down there on the pretext of business because I have a certain . . . curiosity about you, and I wanted to find out more and get to know you better."

Then that feeling that she was somehow on trial, that he was measuring her up against some unknown standard, had not altogether been a mistaken one. Her eyes, direct on his, were silently questioning.

He looked at her for a long moment, deeply absorbed, all amusement gone from his face. Then, with a frown, he seemed to recollect himself.

"Shall we go to dinner now? I'll have to change." He indicated his casual attire. "While I'm gone, you decide where you would like to eat."

"Oh, but I'm not dressed to go either," she protested, looking down at her plain burgundy wool skirt and white jersey top.

"We need not go anywhere dressy, in that case. I would ask you to dinner here but my help is out for the evening."

"I could cook something," she volunteered, and immediately wondered if the offer had been quite proper under the circumstances.

He had no such hesitancy, and when she reassured him she would not mind at all, he seemed to welcome the idea. He led the way to the kitchen through the silent house and Sally was acutely conscious of being totally alone with him.

She started with pleasure at the sight of the enormous kitchen he led her into. Although it had every modern convenience, the room also had an old-fashioned lived-in look. In the center stood a scrubbed wooden table that would have seated a family of twenty comfortably. Over it, suspended on hooks from the ceiling, was a forest of pots, pans, baking dishes, and cooking utensils of every shape and size. The walls were lined with shelves and cupboards holding an awesome array of herbs and spices. The stove and wall ovens looked capable of handling the cooking for a small hotel, and Sally wondered if Hawker did much entertaining in his house. Certainly, judging from the dimensions of the kitchen, the house had been made for it.

He followed her admiring gaze around the room. "You'll have to show me where things are," she said, at once businesslike.

"I haven't the slightest idea where things are," he confessed. When Sally turned to him in amazement, he gave an apologetic shrug. "Don't look at me with such horrible disapproval. I could tell you about every single press we have in the Globe Building but I'm guilty of gross ignorance in my own kitchen. I have a couple who look after the house. The only time I come in here is when I open a can of dog food for old Tom here."

Taking his cue, the dog, who had trotted into the kitchen on their heels, now barked vigorously. Hawker silenced him with a gentle slap on his shiny wet nose.

Sally began to make her exploratory tour around the kitchen while Hawker, looking out of place on a kitchen stool, and Tom, seated at his feet, followed her movements with interest. She soon found the plentifully stocked pantry and in ten more minutes had ingredients and utensils gathered together for a meal.

Only for a moment did the incongruity of the situation occur to her. That the publisher of *The Globe* sat watching her with his elbows on the kitchen table while she was preparing an evening meal for the two of them was hardly in keeping with his fearsome image.

Hawker offered his inexpert help but she waved him aside. Wisely, she decided against showing off with one of her more elaborate dishes and decided on a shrimp and avocado appetizer, steaks, and a Caesar salad. With the familiar job of cooking, her confidence returned, and she was soon engrossed in her work and in the easy conversation that flowed between them.

Only once did she remind herself that this happiness would be short lived, that tomorrow morning she would be just another one of his reporters. Her heart was too full at the moment to pay the warning much heed.

Their conversation centered mostly around her and her family again, but emboldened by the companionable mood between them, she asked suddenly, "Where did you spend your childhood?"

"Right here in New York," he replied without hesitation, adding sardonically, "though not in this neighborhood, I can assure you."

"Do you have any family?" she ventured further.

"No, none that I know of, none that has acknowledged me since I was a kid."

At Sally's quick sympathetic look he gave an ironic smile. "Now don't go breaking your tender little heart thinking that there is a heart-wrenching melodrama attached to my dark past. I don't particularly like talking about it—but for no other reason than it just doesn't interest me very much."

Sally had paused in her work and was looking at him with expectancy. He gave a resigned laugh and capitulated.

"Very well, I can see the tears of compassion will start brimming over at any moment if I don't let you in on the story of my life. But I warn you, you're in for a big letdown. It wouldn't even make a decent sob story for *The Globe*." Briefly and with detachment he told the story.

"My father died when I was nine, and as far as I know, my mother died shortly after. In any case, she disappeared one day and was never heard of again. I couldn't find out whether she was alive or dead when it mattered, and now it doesn't seem to make any difference. I was passed around into various homes for a few years until, at thirteen, I ran off and got myself a job." That, Sally thought, explained his preoccupation with her own close-knit family and what he had meant when he had told her earlier that he spent a lot of time looking through windows like Aunt Emily's when he was a kid.

"I've been working ever since. Along the way I took some calculated risks and bought myself a run-down country newspaper." He paused for a moment before going on modestly. "It happened to work out, so I bought others. There it is." He looked at her with a smile. "I know it sounds positively unromantic and even dull compared to the rumors that have been invented about me, but you asked for it."

Sally knew the story had been greatly over-simplified but guessed that very few others had heard even this much of it. Hawker got up from his stool and stretched himself.

"How does all that fit in with your estimation of me?" he asked, a wry smile playing about his mouth.

"I . . . I haven't made an estimation," she said uneasily and not quite truthfully. "You're still a . . . stranger to me. That mysterious man they call the Hawk." Her gaze was candid.

"Yes, I'm aware that that's what they call me behind my back," he acknowledged, not at all bothered. "That would be quite an off-putting nickname to someone like you."

Before she had time to respond to his questioning glance, the ring of the telephone interrupted. With a look of annoyance he went to pick up the extension on the kitchen wall.

"Yes?" he demanded. She supposed there was no need for him to identify himself; that strong decisive voice would be recognizable to anyone. She herself had lost her composure at the sound of it many times.

Hawker listened silently for a minute, then said tonelessly, "That sounds like an interesting evening, but I'm busy right now. Perhaps we could make it another time. I'll call you some time tomorrow." He hung up without further explanation.

It could have been anyone on the other end, Sally

reasoned, so why did she have to torture herself by imagining that it had been Althea? To no avail, she reminded herself that she had no business feeling as she did at the thought.

In a few more minutes dinner was ready and she suggested they eat it right there in the kitchen. She wanted to prolong the comfortable mood that they had enjoyed there for the last hour.

"Suits me fine," he agreed, "provided you can be persuaded to set your place next to mine instead of at the other end of the table as you would no doubt prefer to do." Why was he insinuating that she was anxious to keep her distance? Had he forgotten how willingly she had come into his arms once already?

While she found plates, knives, forks, spoons, and glasses in various cupboards, Hawker opened another bottle of wine and filled two copious glasses. Over the meal their easy mood returned and the animated conversation made her eyes sparkle and cheeks flush. She felt headily carefree, thanks partly to the relaxing influence of the wine, and laughed a great deal, enjoying his dry humor when she did not find herself to be the subject of it. Now and again she stole a wondering look at him, hardly able to believe that this genial companion was the same man who could, with one cold glance, chill the very blood in her veins.

He complimented her on the meal and added, "Though it hardly comes as a surprise to me that you are an excellent cook. I expected as much after looking around your apartment. You're quite a homemaker."

After the meal he drew her away from the sink as she made moves to wash up, and led her firmly from the kitchen. They returned to the living room, which was now in darkness except for the glow from the still burning fire. Hawker brought new life to it with a couple of fresh logs while Sally walked about the room, pretending to examine the paintings. Now that they had left the kitchen, she felt her confidence rapidly deserting her. This elegant room had an altogether different atmosphere and, apprehensive, she was trying to delay the moment when she would have to join Hawker by the fire.

"You know you can't really see those paintings in this light and I have no intention of turning the lamps on. Why don't you stop pacing about like a trapped gazelle and come and sit down here." His voice held something unfamiliar that set her nerves trembling.

"Perhaps I'd better go," she suggested in an uneven voice.

In a moment he had left the fireplace and was standing beside her.

"You don't really want to go, do you? Tell me you don't want to go, Sally." The rough command of his voice increased to a husky urgency.

Mesmerized by his fiercely glowing eyes, she repeated in a whisper. "No, I don't want to go."

There was a look on his face she had never expected to see there, a look of need and unconcealed desire. Slowly, as if in a dream, she saw his mouth coming nearer, and then he was kissing her insistently. At the first contact they both tensed almost convulsively and she felt the pressure of his crushing lips increase their intensity. For only a second she hesitated, then yielded happily. He tore his mouth away only to return it with renewed urgency. The violence of the feeling that rushed through her made her shudder and, understanding, he protectively drew his arm closer about her. She felt almost dizzy and thought her body was about to snap in half when his embrace slackened and his mouth left hers.

He held her at arm's length and looked at her with burning eyes before his lips descended again to softly caress her throat, one hand stealing down to come to rest on the spot where her heart was beating wildly against her rib cage.

She saw self-imposed control in his face before he smiled and murmured into her hair, "Your heart feels like a captive little bird. You're not afraid of me, are you?"

"A little," she admitted, averting her eyes.

He lifted her chin and forced her eyes to meet his. "Why?" he asked incredulously.

"Because . . ." she hesitated, then blurted out, "because you could hurt me."

"No more than you could hurt me," he said steadily.

She looked at him in utter wonder. She hurt *him*? How could that ever happen? Her heart soared at what she saw in his face. Did she imagine it or was there an open look of yearning there?

"You tell me you're afraid of me, yet you defy me at every turn you can," he said, shaking his head.

The shrill ringing of the doorbell came as a physical shock to both of them. Sally drew away with a start, and a savage look crossed Hawker's face. He remained where he was, giving every appearance of ignoring the sound.

Someone was pushing the bell insistently and Sally felt her nerves jar with each ring. By this time the dog had run into the hall and was barking in accompaniment. "You had better answer it," she appealed to him.

She saw a flicker of anger in his eyes. "I won't be long," he threw over his shoulder.

But these precious moments will probably be gone by the time you get back, Sally's heart cried out.

A familiar, faraway voice came to her now through the open door. As the voice drew nearer and louder, she recognized with a sickening plunge in the pit of her stomach to whom it belonged. The next moment the door was flung wider and Althea burst in, still talking volubly to Hawker, who followed behind her, turning on the light.

"Anyway, I decided to see for myself if you were really busy or if I could persuade you to join us tonight. It really should be a very amusing little party and—" Her voice died abruptly as she caught sight of Sally.

She had never before seen such a mixture of astonishment and venomous hate on anyone's face as distorted Althea's perfect features that moment. The woman stopped in her tracks and her blue eyes blazed cold fire until she finally managed to recover herself.

"Goodness, have I interrupted some sort of business meeting?" she asked with a vivaciousness that did not match her expression.

"No, this was strictly a social meeting. Sally and I have just finished dinner." Hawker appeared amused and Sally wondered if he was enjoying the situation. She greeted Althea politely and was rewarded with a frosty smile.

"I didn't know you were in the habit of entertaining your staff here, Rafe," she remarked, not quite able to keep the malice out of her voice.

For an instant Sally saw Hawker's brows draw together ominously, but the look passed and he said in his drawling, dry manner, "Don't be so superior, Althea. You have dined here too and you are staff, aren't you?"

The displeasure in hearing herself referred to as "staff" was evident from the woman's expression, but she quickly recovered ground.

"Oh, yes, darling, I must say I have had some divine dinners here." She smiled at him coyly, then turning to Sally, asked archly, "Don't you think he has the most marvelous cook?"

"Sally wouldn't know that, Althea," Hawker interrupted her smoothly. "We were alone here tonight and she cooked our dinner. I must say her cooking rivals anyone's."

Althea paled visibly at this revelation but managed to say with an insinuating smirk, "So I believe. Mike Costello has nothing but praise for her cooking. And I think he is an expert on it by now."

It was a well-timed remark and Sally saw the whole evening destroyed in Rafe's returning glance of contempt.

Althea had the satisfaction of seeing a tension spring up between the two, but she was not so pleased with having lost Hawker's attention.

"Rafe, darling," she purred, "I would adore a glass of that magnificent brandy you keep. It's a beastly cold night outside." She shivered prettily, drawing the mink coat, which she had not yet been invited to take off, closer around her.

"Sally? What will you have?" he asked, his voice still coldly controlled.

"Nothing, thank you," she replied stiffly. Where had the evening gone? What had happened in a few moments to destroy the magic of the last few hours? If only Althea had never come. "As a matter of fact, I was about to leave anyway," she added with sudden decision.

"No you weren't," Hawker contradicted, evoking a look of fury in Althea's face.

"I'm going," she told him with quiet defiance, looking squarely at him. She saw his mouth tighten but he only said in reply, "In that case, I shall drive you home."

For the first time since her arrival, the smile on Althea's face was genuine. "I'll just make myself comfortable by the fire and wait for your return then, shall I, Rafe darling?"

Hawker looked at Sally as if to measure her reaction, but she kept her expression closed. He shrugged angrily and said, "Please yourself, Althea."

In the car there was silence, his angry, hers full of misery. She had warned herself at the beginning of the evening that she would have to pay the price for whatever happiness she found tonight, but she had not counted on paying it this soon. When they stopped outside her apartment she expected no more than a cold good night from him, but turning off the motor, he faced her, a hard glint in his eyes.

"May I ask why you decided to run off in this manner tonight?" he demanded.

"That is rather obvious, isn't it?" she replied, swallowing to ease the lump in her throat.

"Well then I must be extremely slow witted because it is not in the least obvious to me. You'll just have to be patient with me and explain why you chose to leave."

"Why don't you ask Althea to explain when you get back?" she heard herself snap, and realized at once how petulantly childish the words sounded.

His scowl turned into a sardonic smile. "So that's it!" he exclaimed. "You don't approve of Althea, so you walk out in a huff. And this from the girl who grows indignant every time I caution her about a worthless person like Mike Costello," he laughed harshly.

Aroused by his sarcasm, she shot back, "You don't have the right to decide for me who is worthless and who is not, not when you . . ." She was going to say not when you have someone like Althea Beecham for a constant companion, but stopped herself.

"Do go on," he prompted with sarcasm.

"No," she shook her head. "I would not be so presumptuous as to criticize one of your friends. You don't even know Mike Costello, yet you have the arrogance to decide he is worthless."

She had no idea why she was suddenly springing to Mike's defense when she actually disliked him and had to agree with Hawker's assessment of his character. She had spoken unthinkingly, angered by the fact that he was so critical of everyone when he seemed totally blind to Althea's negative traits.

She saw his eyes grow cold as he took her by the shoulders and wrenched her to face him. "I know him a great deal better than you obviously do," he said tightly. "I've had the dubious pleasure of his acquaintance much longer than you and though I keep him employed on my paper, I know him for what he really is. However, if you intend to spend the rest of the evening debating Mr. Costello, you can count me out." His grip tightened on her shoulders as his eyes pierced angrily into hers. "You know for a moment there tonight . . . " He shook his head and left the sentence unfinished.

Sally waited, hoping, but he did not go on. He let go of her abruptly and got out of the car. He escorted her to her apartment door without a word, but there he turned to her and said bitterly, "It was a promising evening, Sally. Too bad it did not live up to the promise."

She made a pleading step toward him, but he had already turned and without another word he was gone.

CHAPTER TEN

The days were growing increasingly colder as Christmas was approaching. When Sally broke the news to her aunt that she would not be able to go home for the holidays, Emily Holloway was distraught.

"But darling, you've never been away from us for Christmas before," she cried. "The family has always been together. It just wouldn't be complete without you."

"Yes, Aunt Emily, I know, but the paper still has to be published even though it's Christmas, and since I had Thanksgiving off it's only fair that I be rostered on duty for this holiday," she tried to explain.

"What about that nice Mr. Hawker, dear?" her aunt persisted. "Remember, we invited him for Christmas and he seemed rather pleased with the idea. Surely if he owns the paper he will give you the time off."

"I think he has probably forgotten all about that invitation by now, Aunt," Sally sighed.

"Well, I'm certain if I asked him . . . "

"No, you can't do that!" she cut in with alarm, horrified at the possibility of her aunt ringing him up to beg time off for her. A little more calmly she added, "That would be too unprofessional and unfair to whoever had to take my place." Not to mention unthinkably humiliating for me, she thought.

Her aunt argued the point for a long time, even suggesting the improbable scheme of bringing the whole family to New York if Sally could not come to them.

Sally pointed out the impossibility of this, explaining that she would be too busy working anyway. Reluctantly, her aunt resigned herself to the disappointment that for the first time since she had come to live with them, Sally would not be part of the family circle at Christmas.

"How terribly lonely it will be for you, darling," Aunt Emily lamented. "Be sure and call us so we can cheer you up."

Yes, Sally silently agreed, it would be the loneliest Christmas of her life. Even Margaret and Cathy had managed to get off duty from the hospital and were full of plans for reunions with their families. None of Sally's other friends would be in town either, but as she had told her aunt, she would be busy working anyway, so the loneliness might be easier to endure.

Aunt Emily's reference to the invitation to Hawker stirred the hurt she had been trying to hold at bay. For the past few days, since the evening at his house, she had feverishly waited for a call, a visit, or some sign from him. Every time the telephone rang, her throat constricted as she reached for it with hesitant expectation, only to be disappointed each time. Logic told her it was futile to expect to hear from him, but her heart contradicted her and kept hope alive.

Once again, the evening had ended in complete disaster between them but this time she realized that she herself had been partly responsible. After all, it had been she who had broken it up, marching out of there the moment Althea had arrived. And what stubborn folly had prompted her to taunt him by springing to Mike Costello's defense, a man she had come to despise? She could not forget the look on Hawker's face when he had said, "For a moment there tonight I thought . . . " It was that look that kept hope alive in her despite all the arguments her logic presented.

In the next few days she did some Christmas shopping and made a few small preparations for the holiday. She bought a tiny Christmas tree and a few ornaments, determined to keep some of the spirit of the season alive, and sent presents home to her family.

Party-giving had begun in earnest and *The Globe* staff, through their contact with so many people, were invited to dozens of them. Sally avoided most of the parties, but there were one or two she simply had to attend.

At one of these, just three days before Christmas, she found herself, to her great displeasure, face to face with Mike Costello. The room was too crowded for her to make a quick escape and he successfully cornered her. At once she saw that he had been drinking a great deal and braced herself for an unpleasant encounter.

Either deliberately or because of his inebriated condition, Mike appeared to have forgotten the hostility of their last meeting and looked delighted at having bumped into her. Oh, well, Sally thought with resignation, she couldn't avoid him for the rest of her life; it was inevitable that she cross his path now and again so she might as well make the best of it. She gave him a cool smile but it was enough to give him encouragement and he lurched toward her unsteadily.

"Why, hello, gorgeous," he said, so loudly that Sally winced. "You're just what this party needed. It was getting awfully dull. D'ya come alone?"

Sally told him she had come with two other reporters but had lost them in the crush when they went to get her a drink.

"I had better go and try and find them," she started excusing herself, but Mike held on to her.

"Have mine," he offered, thrusting out his glass clumsily so that half its contents splashed on his sleeve, but he did not appear to notice. "Do you good . . . put some of that lovely color back in your cheeks." Narrowing his eyes critically, he continued loudly over the babble of voices. "You've been rather off color lately Sally. You're not as happy as you used to be. Could it be you've been missing me?" he asked with an unsteady leer.

Sally murmured something evasively, desperately wishing that one of her colleagues would return and rescue her.

Suddenly Mike's voice turned husky and unpleasantly insistent. "You know I've missed you. Missed you awfully, Sal. I don't know what I did or said to make you turn against me like this." His look of hurt was comically out of keeping with his usual bombastic manner and Sally drew back uncomfortably. She was beginning to feel hopelessly trapped and made up her mind to make a hasty disappearance as soon as opportunity allowed.

"You can't really blame me for anything that's happened," he continued in a whining voice.

"Please, Mike, let's not discuss that now. Let's just drop the subject," she urged impatiently.

Mike made no sign of hearing her and went on loudly, so that heads were beginning to turn in their direction. "I didn't think a small misunderstanding like that could destroy our friendship, Sal. It wasn't my fault. . . . It was you who turned your back on me."

His speech was getting increasingly incoherent and Sally realized she had a very drunk man on her hands. She looked around in desperation for some help but, seeing none on hand, decided to leave Mike where he was and make a rapid exit herself.

She started pushing her way through the crowd but Mike held on to a fold of her dress and followed close at her heels. At least she would fight herself clear of the suffocating crowd and find a clear space where she would be able to deal with him more readily, Sally decided. She struggled toward a corner and finally found herself in a little clearing, away from the merrymakers. She turned around to confront Mike and saw with a sinking heart that he was grinning at her expectantly. He seemed to be happily under the delusion that she had fought her way to this corner just to be alone with him.

"Sally," he murmured thickly, leaning perilously toward her. With a gesture of disgust, she pushed him away. His face registered surprise for a second, then he was grinning again.

"Want to give me a little Christmas kiss?" he pleaded, ignoring the look of distaste with which she greeted the suggestion. The next moment Sally felt herself pushed against the wall, and Mike, breathing laboriously, was making an attempt to pin her there. She struggled angrily but unsuccessfully to break free from his hold.

"My, my, what an absolutely lovely picture," a silken voice cut in behind them. Mike turned around to see who the speaker was and Sally took her chance to break free.

"Such an attractive couple, and you suit each other so well," Althea Beecham purred, malicious triumph in her eyes. "How pleased Rafe Hawker will be to hear of the great affection that exists between the members of his staff."

Althea's appearance had an immediately sobering effect on Mike. He stood up straight and glared at her with unconcealed hostility. For a second two pairs of cold blue eyes locked in battle, then Althea's shifted to Sally.

"I'm so glad to see you enjoying yourself, Sally," she sneered. "You look so much happier than the last time I saw you. Of course, you aren't so much out of your element now as you were then. No doubt you find this much more fun than slaving over a hot stove. After all, dear," she added with honeyed sarcasm, "it *is* a rather outdated notion these days that the way to a man's heart is through his stomach . . . especially if the man is Rafe Hawker."

Mike looked puzzled at this smug speech of Althea's but he turned on her angrily nonetheless. "I wouldn't take her advice on the subject of men's hearts, Sally," he said caustically. "The only thing she knows about it is that a man's wallet usually lies somewhere in the area."

Althea shook her head at him pityingly. "You are so tiresomely vulgar, Mike."

"And I've only just began," he warned, "so you had better draw your claws in and run along."

Sally felt panic rising in her. These were the very last people in the world she wanted to be cornered with, and she was not going to stand here caught in a crossfire between them.

"If you two will excuse me," she said tightly, starting toward the door, "this is not my idea of a pleasant evening."

"Oh, I know what your idea of a pleasant evening is," Althea snapped, suddenly all the false brightness gone from her manner.

"I very much doubt that you do, and in any case I don't want to hear your theories on the matter," Sally retorted. She had no desire to let the conversation go further, especially in front of Mike. "Now I really would like to go, if you don't mind." She shook Mike's detaining hand off her arm.

Althea, furious that once again she had failed to provoke the desired reaction from Sally, fired her parting shot.

"In that case I had better wish you a happy Christmas right now," she said. "I won't be seeing you again till after the holidays are over. Rafe and I are leaving tomorrow morning to spend them at my family's estate in the country."

In spite of the sinking feeling inside her, Sally

managed with effort to murmur, "I hope you have a very pleasant time."

"Oh, I will," Althea purred. "You see, Rafe and I plan to spend the time making plans for our engagement."

Afterward, Sally could not remember how she had managed to get out of there. She caught a cab and rode all the way home in a daze, clutching her hands so tightly that her fingernails left angry red welts in her palms. Absently, she gave the driver an extravagant tip and heard his effusive thanks and good wishes for the season follow her all the way to the front door.

The house seemed extremely still and lonely, all but a couple of the tenants being already gone for the holidays. Once in her apartment, she did not turn on the lights but went to one of the windows and looked out. If only this cold drizzle would stop and snow would take its place. She hated the chilling winter rain and longed for the blanket of thick snow which would be covering Glenbrook by now.

Slowly, the pain started welling up. "Rafe and I will be making plans for our engagement." The words hung like a dagger above her heart. They were going to the country together and would probably come back with everything settled between them. Those devastating words rang tauntingly in her mind, mocking every dream, every hope she had clung to.

Why, *why* had she allowed herself to dream and hope? How many times had she warned herself, how many resolutions had she made only to break again at the first sign of tenderness from him? Why could she not have steeled her heart and saved herself this anguish?

It serves you right, she told herself mercilessly. Maybe if she was really hard on herself she could dam the tide of pain that was washing over her. But it was no use. She stood at the window for a long time, looking out with unseeing eyes, her burning forehead pressed against the cool glass.

Gradually she became aware that she was shivering

uncontrollably. A complete weariness stole over her, bringing with it a merciful feeling of numbness. If only this night could be over, if only she could close her eyes on this waking nightmare and wake refreshed.

Undressing slowly, she went into the bathroom and turned the shower on full force. She stood under its cleansing spray for a long time, letting the water run freely over her hair, turning her face up to its beating force. Automatically she scrubbed at her body with a brush until it glowed red, trying to wash away all the sorrow and disappointment.

She had just wrapped herself into a blue terry robe when there was a loud crash against her door. Her hand stopped in midair and her heart beat a violent rhythm while she waited to see if the sound would be repeated.

It came again, this time in the form of a loud knocking. For a second panic seized her. Whoever it was on the other side of the door had somehow gotten past the locked front door without buzzing her. In the next instant she collected herself. If it was a burglar or some other intruder, he would certainly not announce himself by loudly knocking on her door.

Summoning her courage she went toward the door and called out in as firm a voice as she could master.

"Yes? Who's there?"

"It's me, gorgeous," came the slurred, unmistakably drunken tones of Mike Costello.

Her first reaction of astonishment quickly turned to anger as she called out to him. "This time you really have gone too far, Mike. I want you to leave at once and kindly do it without making any more noise!"

"Not till you let me in, Sally. I can't leave until you let me speak to you," he yelled.

She could not engage in a shouting match with him; the one or two neighbors who still remained in the house would surely be aroused and then she would have a full-scale scene on her hands. She had to quiet him somehow. She opened the door slightly to try to deal with him more directly and at once realized her mistake.

His handsome face was distorted by the effect of drink, made grotesque by bloodshot eyes and an ominous leer. He forced the door back and tottered into the room.

"Came to tell you something, Sal," he muttered thickly.

"There is nothing you have to say that I want to hear now or ever again," she told him between clenched teeth, feeling the fury rising in her. "How dare you come here in a state like this? How dare you come here at all!" she demanded.

"Now don't get so high-handed with me," he sneered. "I know someone you'd let in soon enough if he came knocking on your door," he continued. To Sally's alarm, he began taking his tie and jacket off.

Mustering all her self-control, she tried to reason with him. "Now look here, Mike, it's obvious you are too drunk to know what you are doing, let alone what you are saying. But if there is a shred of decency left in you, you will let me take you downstairs quietly and put you in a cab."

"You walked out on me at the party . . . you're always walking out on me," he complained, wagging his head, and Sally realized with sinking hopes that he was beyond comprehending her. She would have made him a sobering cup of coffee but she was afraid to go into the kitchen. If he came after her, the place was far too small to ward him off, and she would be trapped. Her mind raced for a plan to get out of this mess.

He was already kicking his shoes off and weaving toward her bed in the alcove. Sally hurried to intercept him but getting within his reach was another mistake.

He made a grab for her, and as she sidestepped quickly to avoid him, he clutched at empty air and lost his balance, falling backward on the bed, his head hitting the night table with a resounding crash. Automatically, Sally bent over him to see if he had been seriously hurt.

Mistaking her concern for affection, Mike tried to pull her down beside him, but the combination of drink and the blow on the head had taken its toll on his strength and she broke away easily.

"What's the matter," he asked. "You still holding out hope for Mr. Hawker? You heard what Althea said tonight. She told me all about it on the way over here. Face it, Sal, you don't stand a chance with him now, so you might as well . . . "

"What do you mean Althea told you on the way over here?" Sally demanded, suspicion flaring in her. "Mike, Mike!" she cried, shaking him, but it was too late; he had already passed out.

She stared at his inert figure with desperate thoughts racing through her head. Althea. He had said something about Althea on their way over here tonight. Could she have had something to do with Mike being here? Had she purposely dumped him on her doorstep? No, the thought was too absurd; even Althea would not stoop to a thing like that. Besides, what purpose would it serve?

She began to pace up and down as the full impact of her predicament hit her. It was unthinkable that she spend the night in the same apartment with Mike Costello, even if he was unconscious. She simply didn't want to. Looking at the sleeping figure with more aversion than she had ever felt for anyone in her life, she thought how right Hawker had been about the man. What an idiot she had been for defending him. She would simply have to pack a bag and go to a hotel for the night, as late as it was.

As she sat there thinking this plan over, she heard footsteps coming up the stairs. With apprehension she realized that her own front door was still ajar and she made a dash to close it. Holding her breath, she leaned against it, listening to the steps coming closer.

Tension made her jump and she let out a muffled scream when a loud knock sounded on her door.

"Who is it?" she called out, her voice rising with hysteria.

"Rafe Hawker," came the terse reply.

Without thinking twice, she flung the door open, relief flooding through her. Her first impulse was to throw herself into his arms, but the look on his face arrested her.

He gave her one cold glance and his eyes traveled straight to Mike's body sprawled out on the bed, visible from the door. His face was tautly drawn in anger; the fire in his eyes was threatening. For a moment Sally was convinced he would lash out at her but he controlled his rage before he looked at her again.

His lips curled into a cruel smile as his glance took in her robe, wet hair, and bare feet. "I see now how ridiculously out of place my concern has been regarding your association with Mike Costello," he said bitterly, brushing past her into the room. "You must have found it very amusing when I cautioned you about the imprudence of befriending a man like him."

Turning to her with a look of contempt that tore through her, he added, "I must beg your pardon for my unwitting interference. You see, I hadn't realized that things had . . . ah . . . progressed this far between you."

Sally heard the words and saw the expression, but she did not want to believe them. "What are you saying to me?" she asked in a horrified whisper.

"Let's not play that little game again," he said, nodding toward the bed. "You know, if I didn't have that spectacle right before my eyes, I could easily fall for your wide-eyed, blushing innocence again. I must admit, I have done just that several times in the past."

Sally shrank back from him, her green eyes a dark contrast to the pallor that had spread over her face.

He gave her a bitter look and strolled over to the bed. "Peaceful little sleeper, isn't he? Though I must say his inattention isn't very flattering to you." His expression changed to one of disgust as he looked down on the loudly snoring man. "So this is the poor misunderstood man I had libeled so infamously." He shot a glance of barely concealed anger at Sally and said, "It looks like he's out for at least twenty-four hours. What do you intend to do with him?"

Sally shook her head brokenly. "I . . . I already tried to lift him but he was too heavy. I couldn't get him out of here."

"Ah, you want to get him out of here?" he asked with elaborate surprise. "Well, I'll be happy to perform that act of chivalry for you," he said grimly, and without ceremony he heaved Mike off the bed. The drunken man did not even stir as Hawker hoisted him effortlessly on one of his shoulders.

At the door he turned to Sally. "Don't think we've finished yet."

Everything would be all right once she explained to him all that had happened tonight, Sally tried to comfort herself as she sat huddled in a chair. She tried not to think of his savage attack, of the things he had said to her and the way he had looked. The situation must have seemed quite damning to him, she knew, and told herself that was the reason he had reacted with such vehement anger. The main thing was that he was here when she so badly needed him; nothing else mattered.

Patiently, she waited for him to return and soon heard his steps on the stairs.

The explanation she had prepared died on her lips when he came back into the room. The look on his face made her clutch the arms of her chair.

"I have deposited your friend in a cab," he told her in a dangerously controlled voice. "I'm prepared to spend the rest of the night listening to a no doubt fascinating explanation from you but I warn you, you'll need all your powers of imagination to get out of this one." He looked at her through narrowed eyes and added with measured sarcasm, "And try not to resort to your vulnerable act this time. I doubt I'd fall for it under the circumstances."

She had known him to be unforgiving and quick to judge but had hoped that he would at least give her a chance to tell him what had happened before he decided how much of the blame was hers. Now she saw those hopes shattered. He had made it clear that he was not prepared to believe anything she had to say.

Trembling, very near the verge of hysteria, Sally jumped to her feet and cried out, "You don't really want an explanation, do you? As always, you have already decided for yourself. Your arrogance is so unbending that you draw your own conclusions long before the facts are known to you. Well, I won't give you the satisfaction of sneering at my explanation! I won't apologize for things that didn't even happen!"

"You refuse to give an explanation?" Hawker asked tightly.

"I don't owe you one," she cried out bitterly.

His eyes burned with a hint of something that made her breath catch. "I see I've had an entirely wrong approach to you all this time, Sally," he said, reaching out for her, and before she could move he had pinned her against his body with one powerful motion. His mouth came down on hers in a swift cruel movement and she felt the need in him to hurt her. The pressure of his lips was crushing and when he felt her go limp with submission, he increased it until he heard her moan of pain.

He drew away and shook her so her head snapped back and her hair tumbled over her face. "That's how you like to be kissed, Sally, isn't it?" he demanded cruelly. "You don't appreciate those foolish gallant games of self-control I've forced on myself every time I've had you in my arms, do you? No, that's not the dashing Mr. Costello's style at all—and I've had evidence tonight that you prefer his style. Let's see if this matches it."

Again he kissed her with all the ferocious force of his anger, crushing her against him until she felt the blood leave her head and thought she would faint. From her mouth, his hard, seeking lips descended to her throat and she felt the burning touch of strong demanding hands on her bare skin. With a strength born of desperation she wrenched herself free and tried to run from him.

Relentlessly his hand reached out, and in an instant she was imprisoned in his arms again. There was a wildness in his eyes that was completely alien, and seeing it she renewed her struggles to break away.

His laugh was mocking. "And I used to think you were so different, Sally, the one woman I knew who wasn't like all the others." The words were whispered hoarsely, every one of them a fresh stab in her heart.

"But at every turn there has been Mike Costello." The punishing grip of his hands tightened on her. "Which goes to show that you're not so different from the others after all. Except, of course, you do have a rather convincing air of unspoiled innocence and I was easily taken in by it."

She tried to speak then but he stopped her mouth with another suffocating kiss. The kiss which had begun as a gesture to humiliate her suddenly grew demanding, and Sally felt a fire coursing through her body. It was as though his anger had spent itself and desire had taken its place. Her instinct was to meet his demand; she wanted his kisses so much. But not like this. She could not endure them like this. Her heart was too bruised, his words too shockingly etched on her mind, to allow her to submit to his urgency. Again she struggled to be free, and this time he let her go.

A ragged half-sigh, half-sob escaped her. For an instant he looked as if he was moved by her broken sigh and made a move to come to her. Then his face hardened in grim remembrance.

"For the last time, will you give me an explanation?" he demanded.

With the last ounce of self-control and pride left in her, she defied him.

"Never!" she cried.

"That in itself is explanation enough," he said coldly.

"If you think that, then there is nothing we can ever have to say to each other again," she told him quietly.

He turned abruptly on his heels and headed for the door. Before he opened it, he turned once more.

"Forgive me for having forgotten myself, Miss Spencer. I give you my word it will never happen again." She closed her eyes against the chill of his words.

He looked at her for a long moment, then he was gone.

The next day Sally fled New York.

Unthinking and uncaring about her future, she felt only a desperate need to be away from there. Suddenly the city and its associations had become unbearable to her.

She arrived home in Glenbrook unannounced, and at the first sight of her, her aunt became so alarmed that she was ill that she put her to bed at once. Sally immediately sank into a restless sleep that lasted many hours.

The following morning she slipped out of the house before her aunt and uncle had gotten up, while it was still chill and not quite light outside. When she had arrived home, she had told her aunt only that she had been given the holidays off unexpectedly, and Aunt Emily, too anxious over her niece's drawn appearance, did not ask questions. Sooner or later she would have to tell them the truth, but now she needed time alone to think.

She had made her decision to leave New York in the terrible early morning hours after Rafe Hawker had walked out of her life. It seemed the only possible thing to do. She could barely endure another moment in that apartment, and staying on to work at *The Globe* was out of the question. With the dawn, her anguish had subsided into a numbness as she mechani-

cally packed a bag with a few essentials and made a
very early call to Bill McIntire, who was more than
understanding.

Glenbrook was just beginning to come awake when
she left the house, and the snow that had fallen during
the night lay like a thick carpet on the ground. Everything was so quiet and still that Sally felt alone in
the world. Soon the small town would be rising; she
had to get to a quiet spot before people began to
emerge from their houses. To see anyone she knew
and to act cheerful in keeping with the season would
be too much of an effort right now.

The air was frosty and the sky overcast. It looked
like there would be more snow tonight, on Christmas
Eve. She hurried through the quiet streets with Penny,
who had sneaked out of the house with her, skittering
about her feet, darting in and out of bushes and
gamboling happily in the snow.

Huddling into her navy-blue duffel coat with the
hood pulled well forward, she made her way toward
the outskirts of town where the old willow would be
standing bare, except for a crown of sparkling snow. It
would give her a short reprieve before she had to face
her family and maybe time enough to decide what to
do with herself.

The lake was already frozen solid, and it would not
be long before it rang with the excited shouts and
laughter of the local children. How she had loved
this icy playground when she was a child. It gave her
no pleasure now, and she wondered bitterly if her
own heart would ever thaw out again.

Oblivious to the cold, she leaned against the tree
and waited for the comforting tears to come. But the
heavy ache that lay so deep would not be eased, the
relieving tears would not come.

Only six months ago she had stood on this same spot,
but how very different the future promised to be
then. She was about to fulfill her life's dream, and
although she had felt some apprehension, how confi-
dently she had faced the world.

Oh, Rafe! she cried silently.

It was strange, but his engagement to Althea had been forgotten by her until now. She had been in such a state of shock during that night when she last saw him, so preoccupied with the immediate, that she had not remembered he was about to be engaged to Althea. She had been too intent on defending herself against his cruel words to ask questions of her own.

For the first time the extraordinary circumstances of his being in her apartment on that crucial evening occurred to her. Why had he come at that late hour? From his look when she opened the door, it was obvious that he already knew what to expect to see in there. It had to be Althea; it could have been no one else. Mike had planted the suspicion with those few incoherent words before he passed out. But how? And why? She shook her head with resignation. Those questions would probably never be answered now.

What did they matter anyway, now that everything was over? She could never again face Rafe Hawker, not even as an employee, and she was certain he had no desire to see her either, at least not after what had happened between them. For her it would always be a painful reminder, for him probably an embarrassing one. She must not dwell any longer on the reasons for his visit to her apartment that night or on his violent reaction on finding Mike there. She must not allow herself to think of anything but that that part of her life was over, and she would have to make a new beginning.

She had stood still, submerged in her thoughts for so long that the cold was beginning to numb her. Absently, she paced up and down to bring warmth back to her body. If only she could bring warmth back to her heart too. How could he have said those words, how could he have meant them? No, she would not let herself think of them any longer. She would force herself to think of other things, of the holidays, of the future.

Tonight was Christmas Eve, her favorite time of the

year. She had always looked forward to it with the joyous anticipation of a child. As always, there would be the Christmas carolers calling all over town, friends dropping in with presents, and the irrepressible excitement of the children. Utmost self-control would be needed for her to get through the night, and the pretense would have to be carried into tomorrow.

She kept on pacing about the old tree, her eyes on the ground, when Penny, who had been scampering about, suddenly stood still and began a low growl which, turning to a loud bark, finally caught Sally's attention.

She looked in the direction the dog was barking and saw an approaching figure in the distance. She stopped her pacing. Although the figure was still too far to distinguish clearly, there was something about its purposeful stride which made her hold her breath, while a pulse beat in her temple with deafening force.

Mesmerized, as if in a dream, she watched Rafe Hawker making his way toward her through the thick snow. It's a trick of my imagination, this can't be true, she tried to tell herself above the violent thumping of her heart.

But Penny had already darted ahead to investigate the newcomer and was running in excited circles around him, barking uncertainly. Hawker ignored the dog, his eyes fixed on the spot where Sally was standing, still unable to move or make a sign of recognition.

When he reached her, he too stood without saying anything, his eyes searching her face as if he had not seen it in a long time. He saw the purplish dark circles under her eyes and the paleness of her cheeks.

"Forgive me," he said almost inaudibly.

The tears that would not come before now trembled behind her eyes and in her voice.

"What . . . what are you doing here?" she whispered.

"I was invited to Christmas dinner, remember? I didn't want to be late for it." He smiled but his eyes were still serious, searching.

"But . . ." She shook her head incredulously and as she did so a tear slipped down one cheek. He reached out and wiped it away with a hand that was warm in contrast to the chill of her body. She shook her head again, not ready to surrender to a mounting desire to run into his arms.

"The last time . . . all those things you said," she gasped unevenly, fighting to keep down the sobs that were threatening to explode.

"Sally," his voice was husky as he reached out for her, "I can see what those awful words have done to you. If it can be of any satisfaction to you, they have tortured me even more. I regretted them even while I was saying them and they've been haunting me ever since. I've come here to ask you to forgive what I already know is quite unforgivable."

She looked at him, unable to hold off the tears any longer.

"Sally, I love you."

She gave one shaking sob and instantly she was in his arms, his kisses covering her tears and warming her cold, trembling lips. She clung to him, afraid that if she let go the dream would abruptly end. Finally he held her away from him and looked at her.

"I have to know," he murmured. "Can you—*do* you love me?"

"Don't you know that already?" she asked tremulously.

"I have hoped, but time and time again I told myself it was not possible that you could."

"I thought it was the most obvious thing in the world," she cried, and yielded to his encircling arms again. She felt herself soaring to an unimaginable height of happiness as she answered his kisses. Sudden remembrance made her draw away abruptly.

"But what about Althea?" she asked, happiness fading from her face.

"You tell me," he replied, puzzled. "What about Althea?"

"Your engagement to her," she prompted with an anxious frown.

His complete astonishment reassured her at once. "My engagement to her?" he repeated.

"She told me you would be making plans for your engagement during Christmas."

"And you believed her?" he asked. "I really thought you had the lady sized up better than that. I thought you had ample opportunity to learn her devious ways while you worked with her. I also thought you knew me better than to imagine I would get myself engaged to Althea Beecham."

"You believed that I was seriously involved with Mike Costello," she pointed out.

"I never could believe that deep down, but it didn't stop me from feeling furious bursts of jealousy and resentment every time I saw you with him. I couldn't tolerate the fact that you didn't see him for the phony that he is."

"But I did, long before you pointed it out to me, Rafe."

"Then why on earth did you always spring to his defense?" he asked.

"Stubbornness, I guess," she admitted. "And I resented that you criticized him while you were involved with Althea. At least every indication was that you were involved with her."

He took her face in his hands and smiled down at her. "I guess we were both too ready to jump to conclusions about each other. That, my darling, is a definite symptom of love. When you're in love and as unsure about it as I was, you imagine everyone in the role of a competitor."

She looked up at him in wonder. "But I was sure that I gave myself away every time I was with you. I've felt this way about you for a long time, Rafe."

He drew her closer and laughed. "You managed to hide it very thoroughly at times."

"And you, Rafe. You seemed so distant sometimes

and at others so sarcastic and cruel to me," she chided.

"Anyone less naive than you about matters like these, any woman with more conceit than you have, would have recognized my behavior for what it was a long time ago—for the irrational, frustrated behavior of a man very much in love but who is not sure his feelings are reciprocated. And now, my darling, if we don't start back for your house at once, your poor Aunt Emily will be driven to distraction. She was already worried about your disappearance and my sudden appearance this morning. Let's not keep her in suspense any longer."

He rebuttoned his overcoat and, taking one of Sally's hands into his own, led the way back toward town.

"However did you find me here?" Sally asked, puzzled.

"When I arrived at the house early this morning, you had already left. I remembered you telling me about this tree and figured this would be where I would find you. Your aunt looked at me as if I was out of my mind when I asked her for directions to 'an old willow tree by the pond.'"

Sally heard the rest of the story on the way back to the house. It seemed Rafe had not gone into his office on the morning after his encounter with her and had gotten a phone call from his secretary, Eve Tarrant. Bill McIntire had told her that Sally had left and talked of never coming back again. With uncanny instinct, the woman decided to relay this information to her boss.

"She has been looking at me speculatively ever since you first came into my office, and went out of her way to drop your name into the conversation several times. She has been with me for many years and I guess she knows me better than I know myself. She strongly advised me to lose no time in getting back 'a capable reporter like that golden-haired girl,' as she put it. I went to your apartment but you had already gone. So as soon as I could, I drove down here," he concluded.

Sally had been oblivious to everything but his voice and his nearness, and was surprised to see they were already turning the corner into her street. Aunt Emily, who had been watching anxiously for a sign of them, now looked out one of the windows and waved to them.

At the gate, Hawker stopped and turned Sally to face him. "What sort of a chance do you think I stand with your family when I ask them for your hand?"

"The best chance in the world," she told him, her eyes shining with love.

"This will be the first Christmas I've spent with a family of my own in many years, and I'm looking forward to it, Sally," he told her. "But chances are we won't have much time to talk alone for the next day or two. So in case I don't get another chance to say it privately, Merry Christmas, my darling, and let this be the first of countless happy New Years together."

Dell's Delightful
Candlelight Romances

☐ **THE CAPTIVE BRIDE**
   by Lucy Phillips Stewart $1.50   (17768-5)
☐ **FORBIDDEN YEARNINGS**
   by Candice Arkham $1.25   (12736-X)
☐ **A HEART TOO PROUD**
   by Laura London $1.50   (13498-6)
☐ **HOLD ME FOREVER** by Melissa Blakely $1.25   (13488-9)
☐ **THE HUNGRY HEART** by Arlene Hale ......$1.25   .(13798-5)
☐ **LOVE IS THE ANSWER**
   by Louise Bergstrom $1.25   (12058-6)
☐ **LOVE'S SURPRISE** by Gail Everett .... 95¢   (14928-2)
☐ **LOVE'S UNTOLD SECRET**
   by Betty Hale Hyatt $1.25   (14986-X)
☐ **NURSE IN RESIDENCE** by Arlene Hale ...... 95¢   (16620-9)
☐ **ONE LOVE FOREVER**
   by Meredith Babeaux Brucker $1.25   (19302-8)
☐ **PRECIOUS MOMENTS**
   by Suzanne Roberts $1.25   (19621-3)
☐ **THE RAVEN SISTERS** by Dorothy Mack $1.25   (17255-1)
☐ **THE SUBSTITUTE BRIDE**
   by Dorothy Mack $1.25   (18375-8)
☐ **TENDER LONGINGS** by Barbara Lynn......$1.25   (14001-3)
☐ **UNEXPECTED HOLIDAY**
   by Libby Mansfield $1.50   (19208-0)
☐ **WHEN DREAMS COME TRUE**
   by Arlene Hale .... 95¢   (19461-X)
☐ **WHEN SUMMER ENDS** by Gail Everett .... 95¢   (19646-9)

At your local bookstore or use this handy coupon for ordering:

| **Dell** | **DELL BOOKS**
 P.O. BOX 1000, PINEBROOK, N.J. 07058 |

Please send me the books I have checked above. I am enclosing $_____
(please add 35¢ per copy to cover postage and handling). Send check or money
order—no cash or C.O.D.'s. Please allow up to 8 weeks for shipment.

Mr/Mrs/Miss_____

Address_____

City_____State/Zip_____

*A rending story of
the power of love*

Now and Forever

Danielle Steel

author of *Passion's Promise*

In one reckless afternoon of passion, Ian had
shattered Jessica's illusion of their perfect
marriage, and Jessica's bitter taunts were driving
them further apart. Faced with the cruelest
separation a man and a woman can know, Jessica
found that reality can be frightening—or
beautiful.

A DELL BOOK $1.95

Dell Bestsellers

- [ ] **F.I.S.T.** by Joe Eszterhas $2.25 (12650-9)
- [ ] **ROOTS** by Alex Haley $2.75 (17464-3)
- [ ] **CLOSE ENCOUNTERS OF THE THIRD KIND**
  by Steven Spielberg $1.95 (11433-0)
- [ ] **THE TURNING** by Justin Scott $1.95 (17472-4)
- [ ] **THE CHOIRBOYS** by Joseph Wambaugh .. $2.25 (11188-9)
- [ ] **WITH A VENGEANCE** by Gerald DiPego ... $1.95 (19517-9)
- [ ] **THIN AIR** by George E. Simpson
  and Neal R. Burger $1.95 (18709-5)
- [ ] **BLOOD AND MONEY** by Thomas Thompson . $2.50 (10679-6)
- [ ] **STAR FIRE** by Ingo Swann $1.95 (18219-0)
- [ ] **PROUD BLOOD** by Joy Carroll $1.95 (11562-0)
- [ ] **NOW AND FOREVER** by Danielle Steel $1.95 (11743-7)
- [ ] **IT DIDN'T START WITH WATERGATE**
  by Victor Lasky $2.25 (14400-0)
- [ ] **DEATH SQUAD** by Herbert Kastle $1.95 (13659-8)
- [ ] **DR. FRANK'S NO-AGING DIET**
  by Dr. Benjamin S. Frank with Philip Miele .. $1.95 (11908-1)
- [ ] **SNOWMAN** by Norman Bogner $1.95 (18152-6)
- [ ] **RABID** by David Anne $1.95 (17460-0)
- [ ] **THE SECOND COMING OF LUCAS BROKAW**
  by Matthew Braun $1.95 (18091-0)
- [ ] **THE HIT TEAM** by David B. Tinnin
  with Dag Christensen $1.95 (13644-X)
- [ ] **EYES** by Felice Picano $1.95 (12427-1)
- [ ] **A GOD AGAINST THE GODS**
  by Allen Drury $1.95 (12968-0)
- [ ] **RETURN TO THEBES** by Allen Drury $1.95 (17296-9)
- [ ] **THE HITE REPORT** by Shere Hite $2.75 (13690-3)
- [ ] **THE OTHER SIDE OF MIDNIGHT**
  by Sidney Sheldon $1.95 (16067-7)

At your local bookstore or use this handy coupon for ordering:

DELL BOOKS
P.O. BOX 1000, PINEBROOK, N.J. 07058

Please send me the books I have checked above. I am enclosing $_____
(please add 35¢ per copy to cover postage and handling). Send check or money
order—no cash or C.O.D.'s. Please allow up to 8 weeks for shipment.

Mr/Mrs/Miss_____

Address_____

City_____ State/Zip_____

IN 1918 AMERICA FACED AN ENERGY CRISIS

UNCLE SAM **NEEDS** THAT

EXTRA SHOVELFUL

Help Uncle Sam to Win the War

UNITED STATES FUEL ADMINISTRATION

An icy winter gripped the nation. Frozen harbors blocked the movement of coal. Businesses and factories closed. Homes went without heat. Prices skyrocketed. It was America's first energy crisis now long since forgotten, like the winter of '76-'77 and the oil embargo of '73-'74. Unfortunately, forgetting a crisis doesn't solve the problems that cause it. Today, the country is relying too heavily on foreign oil. That reliance is costing us over $40 billion dollars a year Unless we conserve, the world will soon run out of oil, if we don't run out of money first. So the crises of the past may be forgotten, but the energy problems of today and tomorrow remain to be solved. The best solution is the simplest· conservation. It's something every American can do.

ENERGY CONSERVATION -
IT'S YOUR CHANCE TO SAVE, AMERICA

Department of Energy, Washington, D.C